BOB COOK
AND
THE GERMAN SPY

PAUL G. TOMLINSON

Bob Cook and the German Spy

PAUL G. TOMLINSON

© 1st World Library – Literary Society, 2005
PO Box 2211
Fairfield, IA 52556
www.1stworldlibrary.org
First Edition

LCCN: 2004195657

Softcover ISBN: 1-4218-0478-6
Hardcover ISBN: 1-4218-0378-X
eBook ISBN: 1-4218-0578-2

Purchase *"Bob Cook and the German Spy"*
as a traditional bound book at:
www.1stWorldLibrary.org/purchase.asp?ISBN=1-4218-0478-6

1st World Library Literary Society is a nonprofit organization dedicated to promoting literacy by:

- Creating a free internet library accessible from any computer worldwide.
- Hosting writing competitions and offering book publishing scholarships.

Bob Cook and the German Spy
contributed by Tim, Ed & Rodney
in support of
1st World Library Literary Society

CONTENTS

PREFACE --- 7

I. WAR IS DECLARED -------------------------------------- 9

II. THE SECRET SERVICE AT WORK ------------------------ 17

III. BOB HAS A FIGHT ------------------------------------- 25

IV. HEINRICH AND PERCY -------------------------------- 34

V. ON THE BRIDGE --- 40

VI. HUGH HAS AN IDEA ----------------------------------- 49

VII. IN THE NIGHT --- 59

VIII. A STRANGE OCCURRENCE -------------------------- 68

IX. ANOTHER SURPRISE ---------------------------------- 73

X. BOB IS MYSTIFIED ------------------------------------- 83

XI. THE DESERTED HOUSE -------------------------------- 93

XII. TRAPPED -- 105

XIII. MISTAKEN IDENTITY -------------------------------- 113

XIV. AN EXPEDITION ------------------------------------- 126

XV. FIRE -- 134

XVI. MORE COMPLICATIONS ---------------------------- 141

XVII. A MESSAGE --- 150

XVIII. KARL HOFFMANN ---------------------------------- 159

XIX. A DISCUSSION --------------------------------------- 168

XX. ANOTHER SUSPECT ----------------------------------- 173

XXI. ON THE STREET-- 184

XXII. BOB ACTS QUICKLY ---------------------------------- 191

XXIII. UNDER THE LIGHT---------------------------------- 194

XXIV. AT THE FACTORY------------------------------------ 199

XXV. A STRUGGLE IN THE DARK ------------------------ 209

XXVI. AN EXPEDITION IS PLANNED -------------------- 219

XXVII. A RAID AND A SURPRISE -------------------------- 226

XXVIII. CONCLUSION-------------------------------------- 233

PREFACE

Every one knows that Germany is famous for her spy system. Scarcely a land on earth but is, or was, honeycombed with the secret agents of the German Government. Ever since this country began to send war munitions to the Allies an organized band of men has plotted and schemed against the peace and welfare of the United States. When America itself declared war their efforts naturally were redoubled. Our Secret Service has been wonderfully efficient, but it has not been humanly possible to apprehend every spy and plotter at once. It is a big task to unravel all the secrets of this great German organization.

We are at war with Germany now and it is the duty of every American to help his government in every way he can. This book is the story of how two boys, too young to enlist, did "their bit" right in their own home town. It is not an exaggerated tale, but presents in story form what has actually happened all around us. Due allowance is made for the fact that the most of our citizens of German birth and descent are good Americans. No one whose motto is, "America First," need fear offense from anything contained in the story of "Bob Cook and The German Spy." Two boys loved their country and did their duty by it. May we all do as well.

PAUL G TOMLINSON. - Elizabeth, N. J.

CHAPTER I

WAR IS DECLARED

"Well," said Mr. Cook, "I see that the United States has declared war on Germany. I am glad of it, too."

"Why, Robert!" exclaimed Mrs. Cook. "How can you say such a thing? Just think of all the fine young American boys who may be killed."

"I realize all that," said her husband. "At the same time I agree with President Wilson that the German Government has gone mad, and as a civilized nation it is our duty to defend civilization. The only way left for us is to go in and give Germany a good beating."

"And I shall enlist and get a commission," cried Harold, their eldest boy. "I am twenty-three years old. I have been at Plattsburg two summers, and I have done a lot of studying; I know I can pass the examinations."

"What will you be if you do pass?" inquired his father. "A lieutenant?"

"Well," said Harold, "a second-lieutenant."

"I wish I could enlist," sighed Bob.

"Huh!" snorted his older brother. "You can't enlist. What military training have you had? And besides, you're only seventeen; they wouldn't take you."

The Cook family were seated at the dinner table, mother, father, and three children, the two boys referred to above and a young daughter, Louise, just thirteen years of age. Congress had that day declared war on Germany, and naturally that was the one thing in every one's mind. Crowds in front of the newspaper offices had greeted the news from Washington with wild enthusiasm, patriotic parades had been organized, and from almost every house and office streamed the Stars and Stripes.

Bob Cook had been among the crowds, and his young mind and heart were fired with patriotism and enthusiasm. A company of soldiers from the Thirty-ninth Infantry called out the week before had caused him to cheer and hurl his cap high in the air, while all the time he envied the men in khaki.

"I hate to think of you enlisting, Harold," said Mrs. Cook sadly.

"Why?" demanded Harold earnestly. "Don't you think it is my duty to offer my services to my country! I'm free; no one is dependent upon me."

"I know," agreed his mother, "but somehow I don't like to have my boy go over to France and be killed. Let some one else go."

"Suppose every one said that," exclaimed Harold. "We shouldn't have much of an army and our country wouldn't be very well defended, would it?"

"Let him go," said Mr. Cook quietly to his wife. "I don't want him killed any more than you do, but there are some things worse than that. Suppose he was afraid to go; you'd be ashamed of your son then I know."

"How do you know I'm going to get killed anyway?" demanded Harold. "Every one that goes to war doesn't get killed. At any rate it's sort of gruesome to sit up and hear your family talk as if you were just as good as dead already."

"True enough," laughed Mr. Cook. "When does your examination come?"

"Next Monday."

"Will you wear a uniform?" asked Louise.

"Why, certainly," said Harold, swelling out his chest at the thought.

"I wish I could enlist," sighed Bob.

"You're too young, I told you," said Harold scornfully.

"I'll bet I could fight as well as you could," said Bob stoutly. "Besides, I'm big for my age and maybe if I told them I was older than I really am they might take me."

"Don't do that, Bob," said his father earnestly. "Don't lie about it."

"They'd find you out anyway," exclaimed Harold. "You can't fool these recruiting officers."

"I'd like to get to France and see the trenches, and see the soldiers, and the guns, and the fighting," Bob insisted.

"Do you realize that Harold may never get to France even if he does enlist and get a commission?" remarked Mr. Cook.

"Why not?"

"First of all on account of Mexico."

"Do you think the Mexicans will make trouble?" inquired Harold.

"I shouldn't be at all surprised," said Mr. Cook. "If they think we have our hands full with Germany those bandits may stir up a fuss and then troops would have to be sent down there."

"And Harold might be one of them," laughed Bob. "That would be a joke, wouldn't it?"

"I don't see why," cried Harold warmly. "If troops were needed in Mexico and I was one of those sent, I'd be serving my country just the same."

"Of course you would," his father agreed. "It might be though that you wouldn't even get out of High Ridge."

"You think they'd keep us right here?" demanded Harold, his face falling.

"Possibly," said Mr. Cook. "It might be that you'd have your hands full too."

"Do you think the Germans could land an army and invade this country?" exclaimed Mrs. Cook in alarm.

"Not for a minute do I think that," said Mr. Cook.

"Then what do you mean?"

"Aren't there lots of Germans in the country already?"

"Do you think they'd make trouble?"

"Most of them would be peaceable enough, but some of them would only be too glad to blow up some factories, or railroads, or things like that."

"They've been doing that for the last two years," said Harold, "but I don't see what there is in High Ridge."

"There's my company," said Mr. Cook. He was president of the High Ridge Steel Company.

"But you don't make war supplies," exclaimed Mrs. Cook. "Why should they want to blow up your plant?"

"Up until now we haven't manufactured war supplies," Mr. Cook corrected. "This afternoon, however, we took a contract from the Government to make high explosive shells. And, what is more, we are going to do it at cost price so we shan't make a cent out of it."

"I think that's fine," said Bob enthusiastically. "Perhaps you'll have to stay home and guard father's factory, Harold."

"Do you think there'll be any danger to it?" Harold asked his father.

"I don't know," replied Mr. Cook. "There are a lot of rabid Germans in High Ridge and you can't be sure just what they will do."

The telephone rang at that moment and Bob excused himself to go into the next room and answer it. Dinner was now over and the rest of his family shortly followed. As they entered the sitting-room where the telephone was located, Bob was in the act of hanging up the receiver.

"Who was it, Bob?" asked his mother.

"I don't know; it sounded like a German's voice. At any rate he had the wrong number. He said, 'Iss dis Mr. Vernberg?'"

"Oh, Wernberg," exclaimed Mr. Cook. "He's the man who moved into that house down on the corner about two years ago. Karl Wernberg is his full name and he's one of the worst of the Germans; he used to be an officer in the German army, I understand."

"What do you mean 'he's one of the worst of the Germans'?" asked Harold.

"Why, the way he talks against the United States and for Germany. He's made all his money here, too."

"What's his business?"

"Some kind of chemicals, I believe."

"Perhaps he's making bombs," laughed Harold, and the rest of the family joined in the laugh. That is, all but Bob, who took the suggestion seriously, and his heart thumped a beat faster at the thought.

In fact, as he went to bed that night his mind was filled with thoughts of spies, and plotters, and the hundred and one other things connected with the war that he and his family had discussed that evening. He went to the closet and took out the .22 caliber rifle that he owned; it was in good condition and Bob assured himself that he had plenty of cartridges, though he knew so small a gun would be of but little use in time of trouble.

As he undressed he thought over the events of the day. Never had he experienced such excitement. War had been declared, and many of the young men, not much older than he, had enlisted. He, too, wanted to go in the worst way, but he knew that his father and brother were right when they said he would not be accepted.

"Why not?" muttered Bob to himself. "I'm big enough and strong enough too; I could stand it as well as most of those fellows, even if they are older. Besides I weigh a hundred and fifty-three and I'm five feet nine inches tall. Perhaps they won't take me because I've got light hair and blue eyes," he murmured bitterly. "They think I look like a German."

Stripped to the skin he stood in front of the mirror and looked at himself. Certainly he was big and strong. He had always lived a clean, outdoor life, he had been active in athletics and right now was captain of the high school baseball team. The muscles played and rippled under his white skin, as he moved his lithe young body to and fro.

A few breathing exercises before he jumped into bed,

and then he was under the covers. And all night long he dreamed of chasing big fat Germans up and down the streets, over fences, and across fields, and even up the steep sides of houses. Usually just as he had caught up with them he awoke. Most of all he dreamed he was pursuing Karl Wernberg, who was a middle-aged German and not hard to overtake. But Bob did not catch him because he always woke up too soon.

CHAPTER II

THE SECRET SERVICE AT WORK

The following morning Bob was in the trolley car on his way to school. The car was full, and every one was eagerly scanning a newspaper or discussing the war with his neighbor. Words of praise for the President were to be heard on all sides, and enthusiasm was everywhere in evidence. Old men wished they were young enough to enlist.

All at once Bob heard voices raised in dispute. The trouble was at the opposite end of the car, but he could hear plainly what was said.

"It is wrong, all wrong," exclaimed a florid-faced man with a light mustache, who plainly was of German blood. "What has Germany done to this country?"

"They've sunk our ships when they had no right to, and they've murdered our peaceful citizens," said the man next to him. "Isn't that enough?"

"They were forced to do it," the German insisted.

"Oh, no, they weren't," said his neighbor calmly. "Any one can play the game according to the rules if he wants to; there is never any excuse for dirty work."

"Germany wants peace with the United States," said the German loudly.

"Well, if they do, they take a strange method of showing it," replied the other man with a grim smile. "Personally it's my opinion that we've been patient with Germany far too long. Now they've forced war upon us and for my part I'm ready to go out and fight for my country."

Every one in the car was now listening to the discussion, and perhaps the most interested listener of all was young Robert Cook.

"Well, I won't fight for the United States!" exclaimed the big German, rising to his feet. "I won't fight for Germany either, but I'll fight all right." He started toward the door of the car, while Bob pondered over his last remark and wondered what it could mean.

As the German approached the door, a man dressed in a neat black suit and soft hat got up out of his seat. Bob was watching the German and also noticed this man, though not particularly; he did see that he had a square jaw and a determined look in his gray eyes.

The German started to crowd past the stranger who stood squarely in the aisle. "Don't be in such a hurry," said the man quietly. "You stay here."

"I want to get off this car," shouted the German angrily. "Get out of my way."

"I want you to come with me," said the man still in the same quiet tone. As the German started to protest once more he drew back his coat slightly and Bob saw the

Paul G. Tomlinson

gleam of a badge on his coat. "Sit down," he said to the German, who obeyed without further question.

There was a mild flurry of excitement in the car, and there were smiles of amusement on the faces of many of the passengers as they glanced at the German sitting meekly in the corner of the seat. He seemed entirely cowed now, and kept his eyes fixed upon the floor, save for an occasional look he stole at the secret service man standing in front of him. The latter seemed entirely at his ease and acted as if not a thing out of the ordinary had taken place.

Bob was greatly impressed, and looked with marked respect at the quiet-mannered detective standing near him. He wondered what it was all about, and his father's words of the evening before concerning plotters and spies came again to his mind. He wondered if he could join the secret service and help his country in that way. Then he remembered that he was only seventeen and sighed to think that there was probably less chance of that than there was of being taken into the army.

What was the detective going to do with the German, wondered Bob. The car was approaching the high school, and he would have to get off soon and he did not want to miss any of the drama. Suddenly he remembered the police station on the block adjoining the school building and decided that that must be the detective's destination. Bob decided to stay on the car long enough to see anyway.

They passed the high school, and sure enough, as they came to the next corner, the secret service agent motioned to the German to follow him out. Bob decided to go along. They got off the trolley car and entered the police station. Behind the desk sat the sergeant, a man named Riley, well known to Bob. The detective led his prisoner up to the rail.

"I want you to take care of this man for me, Sergeant," he said, at the same time displaying his badge.

"Certainly," said Sergeant Riley quickly. "Here, Donovan," he called to a policeman standing near by. "Take this man and lock him up."

Officer Donovan beckoned to the German who was standing sullenly by the side of the policeman; his face was white and his eyes gleamed wickedly while he opened and closed his hands nervously. He even started to protest, but before he could say anything Sergeant Riley quickly silenced him. Without further ado he joined the policeman, and together they disappeared through the door leading out to the room where the cells were located.

Satisfied that his prisoner was taken in charge, the secret service agent turned and without further ado left the building.

Bob was much excited and interested. "Who was that secret service man?" he inquired of the sergeant.

"Dunno," said Riley. "I never saw him before."

"He didn't even make a charge against the man," said Bob.

"I know it," said Riley. "He don't have to."

"I thought you couldn't lock up a man unless there was some charge against him," exclaimed Bob.

"We have orders to lock up every man them fellers bring in here," said Sergeant Riley. "We keep 'em here until we get word to do something else with 'em. It's not for us to ask questions, you know."

"Have you got any more here?" demanded Bob.

"That's the first; we have accommodations for seventy-five though."

"Whew," exclaimed Bob. "Do you think there'll be much trouble with the Germans here in High Ridge?"

"Can't say. Some of them are a crazy lot. At any rate we're ready for 'em. And what are you doing here at this time o' day anyhow? You'll be late for school; your visiting hour here is usually in the afternoon."

"I saw that fellow on the trolley," Bob explained. "I wanted to see what happened to him."

"Well, you better run along," advised the sergeant. "Come in and see me later."

Bob hurried out and ran down the block toward the high school. His mind was not on his lessons, however. War was uppermost in his thoughts, and he still pondered over what his father had said the evening before, and the recent arrest of the German in the trolley car. Probably after all there was something in this scare about spies and plotters.

He arrived at school fifteen minutes late, but nothing

was said to him. School discipline was greatly relaxed that morning and instead of recitations the first period, the principal gave a talk on patriotism and what the declaration of war would mean. He especially warned the pupils against acting differently toward any of their number who might be of German blood.

"They may be just as good and loyal citizens as we are," he said. "At any rate we must act as though they were until they convince us otherwise."

Bob considered this good advice, but he still thought of his father's words and his experience of that morning. "Suppose anything should happen to father's steel works," he thought. They were making shells for the Government and could afford to run no risks. "I'll see if I can be of any help in protecting them," he told himself.

He tried to concentrate his mind on his tasks, but it seemed hopeless. The words of the German in the trolley came back to him continually - "I won't fight for Germany. I won't fight for the United States either, but I'll fight all right." What could he have meant? Did he mean that he wouldn't try to enlist in either the German or American armies, but that he'd do his fighting on his own account? How could that be? Bob wondered if the fighting he would do would be for this country or Germany. If for this country, it seemed queer that the secret service officer should have arrested him. The thought of bombs returned insistently to Bob's mind.

Recess came at last and he sought out Hugh Reith, his best friend. Hugh was a boy of Bob's own age, almost exactly his size, and as they both liked to do the same

Paul G. Tomlinson

things they were bosom companions. Bob was light and Hugh was dark, his hair was almost raven black, and his eyes a deep brown. He had large hands and several crooked fingers owing to the fact that he had broken them playing base ball. He was stronger than Bob, though not so agile or quick on his feet, and while he could defeat his light-haired friend in tests of strength he was not a match for him when it came to speed.

"What do you think of this war, Hugh?" Bob asked eagerly.

"I wish I could enlist," said Hugh.

"So do I, but I guess we can't."

"We're too young, I suppose. Isn't there anything we can do to help?"

"My father thinks we may have trouble with the Germans here in town. If anything starts you can be sure I'm going to get in it if possible."

"Say," exclaimed Hugh, "did you see young Frank Wernberg this morning when the principal was making his speech about patriotism?"

"No, what was he doing?"

"Oh, he was snickering and making side remarks to Jim Scott, and making himself generally objectionable."

"If I'd been Jim I'd have told him to keep quiet," said Bob warmly.

"That's just what he did do finally."

"Did he stop?"

"Oh, for a little while," said Hugh. "He was awful, I thought."

"You know," said Bob, "my father says that Mr. Wernberg is about the most rabid German in High Ridge. He's crazy on the subject."

"Who, your father?"

"No, Mr. Wernberg. He's crazy on the subject of Germany. He thinks it is the greatest country in the world and that every one in the United States is a fool or something."

"Why doesn't he go back to Germany then?" demanded Hugh angrily.

"That's what I - "

"Sh," hissed Hugh. "Here comes Frank Wernberg now."

CHAPTER III

BOB HAS A FIGHT

Frank Wernberg was a stocky, light-haired boy with blue eyes and a pink and white complexion; that is, it was usually pink and white, though this morning his face was flushed and red. His eyes had a glint in them not usually apparent and his mouth was drawn down at the corners into a scowl. His hair, close-cropped, seemed to bristle more than was its wont; in fact his usual mild-mannered appearance had given way to one of belligerency.

"Hello, Frank," said Bob pleasantly.

"Hello," said Frank shortly.

"What's the matter?" inquired Hugh. "You seem to have a grouch."

Something was in the air and the boys felt uneasy in one another's presence. Usually they laughed and joked incessantly, and Frank Wernberg was one of the jolliest boys in the school. He was inclined to be stout and like most fat people was full of fun as a rule. This morning, however, his demeanor was far from happy.

"Why shouldn't I have a grouch?" he demanded

angrily. "I've just been talking to that chump, Jim Scott. He seems to think that any one who disagrees with him must be wrong."

Bob nudged Hugh. "What was the argument?" he asked.

"The war," said Frank bitterly. "I said I thought Germany was all right, and he tried to lecture me about it. Hasn't a fellow a right to his own opinion?"

"Sure he has," exclaimed Bob. "Any one can think Germany is all right if he wants to, but no one who is an American can side with Germany against the United States at a time like this."

"Who says they can't?" demanded Frank flaring up.

"I say so," exclaimed Bob.

"Who are you to tell others what they can do?"

"I'm an American, anyway."

"Well, I'm a better American than you are," cried Frank hotly.

"And you stand up for Germany now?"

"I do, because Germany is right and America is wrong."

The three boys were standing in one corner of the school yard, removed from all the others so that the rapidly rising tones of their voices passed unheard. Their faces were now white and their breath came fast.

Hugh had taken no part in the argument thus far, but he stood shoulder to shoulder with Bob, prepared for any emergency.

"And what's more," exclaimed Frank, "this country was forced into war by a lot of men who want to make money out of it."

"You're crazy," said Bob.

"No, I'm not crazy either. Some of those men live right in this town too. I guess you know who I mean all right."

"What do you mean?" demanded Bob in a tense voice. "Name somebody. I suppose the fact that Germany has murdered a lot of Americans has nothing to do with our going to war."

"Certainly not," said Frank. "It's the men who want to make money."

"Who says so?"

"I say so, and so does my father."

"Huh!" sniffled Bob. "Name one of the men."

"They may get fooled," said Frank darkly. "Something might happen to their factories and they'd lose money instead of making it."

"What do you mean by that?"

"Oh, you know all right."

"He hasn't named anybody yet," Hugh reminded his friend.

"That's right," exclaimed Bob. "Who are they, Frank?"

"Well," said Frank, "one of the men who thinks he is going to make a lot of money but who may get fooled is -"

"Go on," urged Bob, as Frank hesitated.

"Your father!" snapped Frank suddenly.

Quick as a flash Bob's right arm shot out and his clenched fist caught Frank squarely on the nose. Hugh started forward as if to help his friend, but Bob waved him aside. "This is my affair," he panted.

Whatever else he was, Frank was no coward. Blood was already trickling from his nose and the force of the blow he had received brought tears to his eyes. He recovered himself almost immediately, however, and with head down rushed at Bob. Bob was waiting for him and sent a crushing blow to his opponent's jaw. Again Frank staggered back, but a moment later advanced for more.

He was more wary this time, however, and several of Bob's blows missed their mark. The boys danced about, each sparring for an opening. They were of almost equal size and weight, though Frank was probably a better boxer. Bob, however, was furiously though quietly angry, and convinced that the right was on his side had an advantage to that extent. Meanwhile the rest of the boys, attracted by the noise of the combat were running from all directions to get a close view of the fight. They quickly formed a ring around the two combatants and urged their favorites on. Most of them cheered for Bob, he being popular with all, while Frank had not so many friends.

Bob lowered his guard for an instant, and Frank was quick to take advantage of the opportunity offered. He dealt Bob a staggering blow directly over the left eye; a ring on his finger broke the skin and blood flowed into Bob's eyes, while a swelling appeared almost immediately. He felt no pain, however, and with a yell of rage he rushed at his opponent. He had thrown caution to the winds and consequently Frank drove home two more good stiff punches to Bob's wet and bleeding face. Nothing daunted Bob clinched and swaying back and forth for a moment they presently fell to the ground. Over and over in the dust they rolled, each one trying desperately to get his arms free. The crowd cheered wildly and moved back to give more room to the fighters.

Presently the spectators saw that Bob was on top. He was in better physical condition than Frank and this fact was beginning to count. Frank was short of wind and puffing hard. Bob sat astride him, holding him pinned to the earth with both knees while he pounded his head up and down on the ground.

"Lemme up," said Frank weakly.

Bob bumped him once or twice more for good measure. "Had enough?" he asked.

"Yes," gasped Frank, while the spectators yelled their approval.

Suddenly the cheering stopped and a gap appeared in the ranks of the onlookers. The principal of the school came running toward the spot where the fight had occurred.

"What does this mean?" he demanded, much out of breath.

The two fighters picked themselves up slowly. They were smeared with dirt and blood. Bob's collar was torn and Frank's coat was almost ripped from his back. Bob's left eye was half closed and rapidly turning black; Frank's nose was swollen and the skin all scraped off the side of his jaw.

"We had a fight, sir," said Bob.

"So I see," said the principal, while the crowd snickered.

"He started it," exclaimed Frank.

"I did not," cried Bob hotly, turning half way around as if he was considering pitching into his opponent again.

"We won't discuss that question here," said the principal. "The best thing for you two boys to do is to get cleaned up and then come and see me in my office."

He turned away, slowly followed by Bob and Frank and all the rest of the spectators. "Good boy, Bob," whispered Hugh in his friend's ear. "You did him up all right and he deserved it too." Many others also took occasion to show Bob that they heartily approved of what he had done.

Paul G. Tomlinson

A short time later Frank and Bob stood before Mr. Hewitt, the principal. He was a kindly man and well liked by all the boys, even if they did love to imitate the way he had of looking at them over his spectacles. He was always fair to every one and the boys knew they could expect to be treated justly by him at all times. They respected him and looked up to him.

"Well, boys," said Mr. Hewitt, "I'm sorry you had a difference of opinion."

"That's just what it was, sir," exclaimed Bob quickly.

"Haven't I a right to opinion?" demanded Frank.

"What is your opinion?" inquired Mr. Hewitt.

"Well," said Frank slowly, "I say that the United States is wrong about going to war with Germany."

Mr. Hewitt glanced at Frank over his spectacles. "I'm afraid I can't agree with you, Frank," he said. "I don't like war and I don't believe many of our people do either. There is a limit to any country's patience, however."

"Some people here want war," said Frank.

"Yes," exclaimed Bob. "He said that my father wanted war so he could make money out of it."

"He's making ammunition for the Government," Frank exclaimed.

"But at cost price," said Bob. "He will lose money if anything."

"I have always regarded Mr. Cook as one of our best citizens and a fine man," said Mr. Hewitt. "I think you must be wrong, Frank."

"I tried to convince him that he was," said Bob, stealing a sidelong glance at Frank's battered features. Mr. Hewitt also looked at Frank and a faint smile flitted across his face.

"People should be careful about what they do and say these days," he advised. "You are very wrong to talk against the United States, Frank."

"I only repeated what my father says," exclaimed Frank. "He knows."

"I'm sure he's mistaken this time," said Mr. Hewitt quietly. "I also hope he won't talk like that again; people's feelings are easily aroused in times of war and he might suffer harm."

Frank looked sullenly at the floor and said nothing. Bob held out his hand to him. "Let's shake hands," he said. "We all ought to work together now. I'll forget this morning if you will."

Frank made no move. "Come on, Frank," urged Mr. Hewitt. "Do as Bob says, and in the future try to remember that you were born in America, not in Germany. You were born here, weren't you?"

"No, sir," said Frank. "I was born in Germany."

"Well, at any rate remember that you are living in the United States. Shake hands and go back to your work, and I hope you will have no further trouble."

Frank somewhat reluctantly shook hands with Bob and they walked out of the principal's office together. At the door of the study room Frank turned to Bob. "I shook hands with you then because I had to," he snapped. "I warn you though, I'll never do it again, and you'll be sorry for what you did to me this morning. Yes, you and your whole family!"

Bob was completely taken aback by this sudden outburst but before he could make any reply Frank was gone. Bob walked slowly to his desk, carefully avoiding the glances of the many boys in the room who looked curiously at him and his black, swollen eye.

When school closed that afternoon he hurried away as quickly as he could, for he had no desire to discuss the matter with his schoolmates. Around the corner he waited for Hugh and together the two boys started homeward.

"What did Mr. Hewitt say?" asked Hugh.

Bob told him.

"Good for him," exclaimed Hugh. "What did Frank think of that?"

"He was mad," said Bob, and he told his friend of the threat Frank had made. Hugh was silent for some time.

"We must watch him pretty closely," he said at length.

"Yes," Bob agreed, "and his father too."

CHAPTER IV

HEINRICH AND PERCY

"Bob!" exclaimed Mrs. Cook as her son arrived home that afternoon. "What have you been doing to get that black eye?"

Bob related the story of his fight with Frank Wernberg. He did not tell her of the threat Frank had made against him and his "whole family," however, for he had no desire to cause any alarm. His mother listened with a troubled countenance.

"Oh, Bob," she said. "I wish you wouldn't fight like that."

"But he insulted the United States, and father too," Bob insisted.

"I know," she admitted. "Still I hate fighting so. One boy in the family is enough to worry about."

"Where is Harold?" exclaimed Bob.

"Down at the armory," said Mrs. Cook. "I wish it was all over."

"I wonder if I can go down and see him," said

Bob eagerly.

"Perhaps," said his mother. "I don't know." She turned away and Bob hurried out of the house and turned his steps towards the garage. His plan was to get his bicycle and ride down to the armory. He entered the garage just in time to see Heinrich, the chauffeur, stuffing a large roll of bills into his pocket.

"Whew, Heinie!" he exclaimed. "Where did you get all the money?"

Heinrich seemed much embarrassed at being thus interrupted and colored violently. "Golly," said Bob, "I never saw so much money in all my life."

"Dot's not so much," said Heinrich. "Besides it iss mine."

"I didn't say it wasn't," laughed Bob.

Heinrich Muller was the Cooks' chauffeur. He was a German, as his name implies, but he had been in the United States for over twenty years and had originally come into the employ of the Cook family as a coachman. Then when the automobile had taken the place of the horse to such a large extent he had been converted into a chauffeur.

He was a mild mannered, quiet little man, and had always been a prime favorite with the children of the neighborhood. He could do wonderful things with a jackknife and the whistles, canes, swords and other toys he had made for the Cook children had often filled their friends with envy. He wore thick glasses with gold rims and was very bow-legged. He always said that his legs were crooked because he had ridden horseback so much when he was a young German cavalry trooper.

He was a skillful man with horses, and had never liked an automobile half as much. He loved all animals and they seemed to love him too. At the present time his pets consisted of a small woolly dog, an angora cat, a parrot, and an alligator. The last named pet he kept in an old wash tub, half full of water, and called him Percy. He used to talk to all his pets as if they were human beings, Percy included, and many people had ventured the opinion that his brain was not quite as good as it should be.

"A little bit cracked, but harmless and faithful," was the way Bob's father described him.

Bob had never seen Heinrich so upset as he was that afternoon. He put the rolls of bills in his pocket and looked at Bob fiercely through his thick glass spectacles. His watery blue eyes looked almost ferocious.

"What do you want here?" he demanded.

"My bicycle," said Bob.

"It iss got a puncture," said Heinrich.

"Oh, Heinrich," Bob exclaimed. "Why didn't you fix it?"

"I had no time so far."

"I need a new one anyway," said Bob, looking at his

wheel where it rested against the wall of the garage. "This one is six years old."

"It iss one bunch of junk," said Heinrich.

"Right you are," laughed Bob. "I tell you what, Heinrich; you've got a lot of money now, why don't you buy me a new one for my birthday?"

"Dot iss my money," said Heinrich insistently.

"Of course it is," exclaimed Bob. "You don't suppose I thought for a moment that you stole it, do you?"

Heinrich glanced at him questioningly. "Come and see Percy," he said, apparently very anxious to change the subject.

"What has he done lately?" asked Bob.

"He iss grown."

They approached the tub where the alligator was kept. "I can't see that he has grown much," exclaimed Bob. "He looks about the same to me."

"He iss now two feet and one inches long," said Heinrich proudly. "He does not grow fast though."

"I wish my bicycle was fixed," sighed Bob. "I wanted to ride down to the armory."

"Harold iss in the army," said Heinrich.

"I know it," said Bob. "I wish I was too."

"You want to fight?" Heinrich asked.

"Of course I do. Don't you? You're an American citizen, aren't you, Heinie?"

"Yes, indeed," said Heinrich quickly. "For twelve years I been one."

"You're all right," exclaimed Bob heartily. "If all Germans were as loyal as you I wouldn't have this black eye right now."

"A German hit you?"

"He ought not to be a German, but he is," said Bob bitterly.

"Who was it?"

"I won't tell you. What's the use?"

"It was Frank Wernberg," said Heinrich.

Bob looked curiously at the chauffeur. "How do you know?" he demanded.

"Was it him?"

"Yes, but how could you find it out so soon?"

"Mebbe I guess," said Heinrich.

"Probably you did," laughed Bob. "What do you know about the Wernbergs anyway, Heinie?"

"Nothing," said Heinrich quickly and he acted as

though he had made a mistake. "Look at Percy," he exclaimed. "He iss going down into the water."

The alligator slipped slowly off the rock where he had been dozing. He slid quietly into the water and remained floating there all its four feet standing straight out.

"He iss cute," said Heinrich proudly.

Bob had never considered an alligator as being cute, but he did think "Percy" was interesting. Little did he dream how much more interested he would be in the small animal before many days had passed.

CHAPTER V

ON THE BRIDGE

Harold came home for dinner that night. He was serving in the ninth infantry as a private until such a time as he should pass his examination and receive his commission.

"Bob has seen active fighting sooner than you have, Harold," laughed Mr. Cook glancing at his younger son's battered eye.

"Yes, and he won the battle too," said Bob warmly.

"All I can say is," remarked Harold, "that Frank Wernberg must be an awful looking sight if he's worse than you."

"He is," said Bob. "You ought to see his nose."

"Don't talk about it," urged Mrs. Cook. "I hate it."

"All right," laughed her husband. "Tell us what you have to do down at the armory, Harold. You were lucky to get off to-night."

"Oh, I've got to go back," said Harold. "We'll probably be ordered out for guard duty to-night. I may be guarding your plant for all I know."

"I hope we'll need no guards," said Mr. Cook earnestly. "In spite of all I said last night I can't believe that many people will be disloyal."

"Some German got on our wire by mistake again to-day," said Louise. "He wanted Mr. Wernberg just as that man did last night."

Mr. Cook shook his head slowly. "I don't like that man Wernberg," he said.

"Oh, the secret service must be watching him," said Bob. "They seem to be ready for anything," and he related what had taken place in the trolley that morning when he was on his way to school.

The telephone rang and Bob answered it to find Hugh Reith on the wire. He wanted Bob to go down to the armory that night and see the soldiers. Bob readily agreed.

A short time after supper Hugh arrived at the Cooks', and the two boys accompanied by Harold set out. They felt very proud to be walking with a real live soldier, a man in the olive drab uniform of the American Army. Harold carried a rifle, with an ugly looking bayonet affixed to the barrel, the whole thing being nearly as tall as he was.

The roll call had been started at the armory and Harold took his place in line just in time to answer to his name. Bob and Hugh looked on from the gallery and were greatly impressed by the business-like appearance of the men, and the curt, crisp orders of the officers. The soldiers were divided into squads and presently were marched out of the building to unknown destinations.

"I guess it's all over," remarked Hugh.

"Looks so," Bob agreed. "It's early yet though and I don't want to go home."

"Nor I. What do you say to a walk down by the river? My canoe is in Brown's boathouse and I'd like to take a look at it. It has been laid up all winter and I'll want to get it out pretty soon."

"All right," said Bob. "How shall we go?"

"We can take a short cut down over the railroad bridge."

"Come ahead."

They set out through the streets of High Ridge. Few people were stirring and nowhere were any signs of war. The soldiers had disappeared and the quiet town seemed far removed from the strife of conflict. It seemed incredible that even at that moment some one might be plotting to overthrow the law and order of the little city. It was a far cry to the crimson-stained battlefields of France.

"No school to-morrow," said Hugh finally.

"That's true," exclaimed Bob. "I had forgotten that this is Friday."

"Nothing to worry about," said Hugh. "No lessons to

prepare and as far as I am concerned I'd just as soon stay up all night."

"We ought to have baseball practice to-morrow," said Bob. "Somehow I've lost all interest in it though; this war is more exciting to me."

"If we could only do something," sighed Hugh bitterly.

"Where do you suppose those soldiers went?"

"Out for a hike probably. They looked fine, didn't they?"

Bob said nothing; both boys were busy with their thoughts and walked along in silence for some distance. Presently the steel span of the great bridge across the Molton River loomed ahead of them in the darkness.

"There's the bridge," Bob exclaimed.

It appeared ghostly in the dark, the big steel girders taking on weird and fantastic shapes. A train rushed across its span, roaring and throwing a shower of sparks high into the air.

"Come on," urged Hugh and scrambled up the embankment.

Bob followed close at his heels and together they made their way towards the bridge itself. They soon found themselves picking their way on the open ties above the water; as they were headed west they of course took the east-bound track. The walking was precarious and they had to pay close attention to what they were doing, for a misstep might prove fatal.

Suddenly a sharp command to halt startled the two boys. They stopped short and peered intently about them in the dark.

"Who are you?" demanded a curt voice, and Hugh and Bob saw the figure of a man in khaki outlined against the skyline. A faint flicker of light showed a keen-edged bayonet affixed to the gun he carried.

"Who are you!" repeated the voice, strangely familiar in tone to both of the boys. "Come over here, and keep your hands over your head."

"Harold!" exclaimed Bob suddenly. "Is that you?"

"That you, Bob?" queried Harold, for the guard proved to be Bob's older brother. "Who's that with you?"

"Hugh."

"Well, it seems to me you two are pretty nervy," said Harold testily. "What are you doing down around here anyway?"

"We were going down to Brown's boathouse to see Hugh's canoe," Bob explained. "We thought we'd take the short cut over the bridge."

"And stand a good chance of getting shot," said Harold. "All bridges are guarded by soldiers with rifles, and we're not supposed to wait forever before we shoot either." Hugh and Bob had advanced to the spot where Harold was standing, and the three young men were grouped in a small circle.

Paul G. Tomlinson

"We never thought of that," said Bob sheepishly.

"Don't you know the United States is at war?"

"Of course we do."

"Well, then -. Sssh!" hissed Harold suddenly.

He peered intently down the railroad track. The figure of a man could be seen approaching. "Get back, quickly," whispered Harold, and the two boys flattened themselves against one of the big steel girders.

Nearer and nearer came the man. Harold stood motionless, his gun half raised and ready for instant action. Hugh and Bob looked on, fascinated. When about thirty yards distant the man stooped and appeared to be fumbling with something at his feet. Only for a moment, however, for he soon straightened up again and proceeded on his way.

"Halt!" commanded Harold sharply.

The man started, and then came to an abrupt stop.

"Come over here," Harold ordered.

His order was obeyed somewhat slowly, but without question.

"What's your name?" queried Harold, as the man came up to him.

There was no answer.

"What's your name?" repeated Harold shortly.

"John Moffett," said the man sullenly.

"Where do you live?"

"High Ridge."

"Where in High Ridge?"

"Elm Street."

"What number?"

"Twelve eighty-two," said the man after a moment's hesitation.

"What are you doing on this bridge?"

"I been across the river to see my brother."

"Why didn't you take the passenger's bridge then, instead of this?"

"This one is shorter for me."

"Oh, no, it isn't," said Harold quickly. "The other one takes you right into Elm Street."

The man offered no comment.

"Why did you bend over down there a minute ago?" Harold asked.

No answer was forthcoming.

"Answer my question," ordered Harold curtly.

The man shifted uneasily from one foot to the other. "My shoe lace came undone," he muttered finally. All the time he was talking he kept looking behind him and over the route he had just come. He seemed to be intensely nervous about something.

Harold looked at him up and down from head to foot, as best he could in the poor light. He appeared undecided as to what he should do.

"You'd better come along with me," he said finally. "I guess the captain might like to talk to you for a few minutes."

"Where is the captain?" demanded the man.

"That's nothing to you," said Harold. "You do as you're told. You walk on ahead of me and don't try any funny business; I'll be right behind you and my gun is loaded."

"Which way?" the prisoner asked.

"That way," directed Harold, indicating the High Ridge end of the bridge with the point of his bayonet. "As long as you live in High Ridge I'll see you part way home," he added drily.

"Yes, sir," exclaimed the man, it seemed almost joyously. He set out immediately, Harold following close at his heels.

"You two better go home," Harold called to Bob and Hugh as he walked off down the track.

"All right," called Bob, and then he turned to his

friend. "We'll take our time," he announced.

"Sure," agreed Hugh. "Who do you think that man was?"

"I don't know, but he did act sort of queer I thought. Probably Harold was wise to arrest him."

"What'll they do with him?"

"Oh, lock him up probably," said Bob carelessly. "I guess some officer will question him and if he's all right he'll be let go; otherwise I don't know what will happen to him."

"How about the canoe?" suggested Hugh.

"You mean, shall we go on to the boathouse?"

"Yes."

"The other end of the bridge is probably guarded too," said Bob. "We would be held up there and maybe be arrested ourselves." He peered earnestly down the track which led over the bridge to Rivertown on the opposite bank. Suddenly he started violently and clutched Hugh by the arm.

"What's that?" he gasped in a terror-stricken voice.

CHAPTER VI

HUGH HAS AN IDEA

"What's what?" demanded Hugh, peering in the direction Bob indicated.

"Look!" cried Bob.

"I am looking. What is it?" The tone of his friend's voice had alarmed him greatly, though he did not know what it was that Bob saw.

"Can't you see? Right down there!"

"Where? Where?" pleaded Hugh. "Tell me, Bob."

"Down under the track. I see sparks."

"It's a bomb," cried Hugh suddenly catching sight of the little flashes of light. "It's a bomb that man planted there."

"What shall we do?" cried Bob, acting as if he was ready to turn and run.

"Go and get it," said Hugh instantly. "Come along," and he started towards the spot of danger. Spurred on by his comrade's show of courage, Bob followed.

Their hearts were in their throats and terror held them in its grasp as they hurried along. The little sparks still appeared, and the sputtering of the fuse could be heard distinctly as they ran forward. The footing was dangerous and who could tell but that at any moment the bomb might explode and blow them into eternity.

Hugh reached the spot first. He was outwardly calm, but had the sun been shining his face would have shown white and frightened. A second later Bob arrived and stood beside him.

"There it is," he gasped. "It's a bomb all right."

"Pinch the fuse," cried Hugh excitedly. "Put it out."

Both boys reached for it, but Bob was first. He had completely recovered his nerve now and was perhaps even more self-possessed than Hugh.

Bob grasped the lighted part of the fuse between the thumb and forefinger of his right hand. He squeezed it tightly, but quickly withdrew his hand with a cry of pain. The fuse still sputtered.

"Let me!" almost sobbed Hugh. "Let me try."

He repeated Bob's performance, except that he held on in spite if the pain he suffered. With tight-shut lips and set jaw he pinched the fuse with all his strength. Finally he could stand it no longer and let go.

"It's out," cried Bob. "No, it isn't either," he exclaimed a second later as the fuse once more showed red and the tiny sparks again made their appearance. "We'd better run for it, Hugh. What's the use in our being blown up along with the bridge?"

"Get out of the way!" ordered Hugh, and Bob obeyed at once. There was something in the tone of his friend's voice that made him hasten to do as he said.

Hugh knelt on the ties and leaned down over the bomb.

"Here comes a train," cried Bob suddenly. "On this track too."

Hugh paid no attention to this warning. He picked the bomb up in his two hands and staggering under its weight, carried the spitting and sputtering engine of death to the edge of the bridge. With a supreme effort he hurled it from him. A moment later a splash told that it had landed in the river below.

"That'll never do any more harm," he gasped faintly.

"Stay there, Hugh!" shouted Bob. "Look out for the train!"

The two boys crowded close against the side of the bridge and a moment later a heavy train thundered past them. Through the lighted windows could be seen crowds of passengers, and Hugh and Bob shuddered as they thought what might have happened to the train with its load of precious human freight had the bomb exploded. They felt faint and weak after their experience and presently sat down until their shattered nerves should have recovered somewhat from the shock.

The night was cool, but Bob mopped his perspiring brow. "Whew," he gasped. "That was a close call."

"I should say it was," echoed Hugh. "What luck that you should have seen those sparks when you did! There was only a couple of inches of fuse left."

"Lucky you were with me too," said Bob soberly. "If I'd been alone I think I would have run for home."

"Haven't you two gone home yet?" demanded a voice, and the two boys looked up to see Harold standing over them.

"Not yet," said Bob.

"Well, you'd better skip," Harold advised. "You'll get in trouble around here."

"There'd been more trouble if we hadn't been here," said Bob quietly.

"What do you mean?"

Bob related the story of the bomb to his brother.

"Say!" exclaimed Harold in an awestruck voice. "That was pretty good work of you two. A train came along on that track too."

"Hugh got the bomb out just in time," said Bob.

"Say," repeated Harold. "Say," he said again, completely overcome.

"Do you think they'll let us enlist on the strength of what we did?" Hugh asked hopefully.

"I doubt it," said Harold. "I'll certainly speak to the

Paul G. Tomlinson

captain about you though."

"We might as well go home now, I guess," said Bob. "You don't want to see your canoe tonight, do you?"

"No," replied Hugh grimly. "I've lost all interest in canoes for the present."

They said good night to Harold and started homeward. They still felt a little shaky as a result of the bomb episode, but before long the walk and the crisp night air had refreshed them and their spirits once more revived.

"I wonder what they'll do to that German," exclaimed Bob.

"Harold said they had locked him up for over night, and I guess when they hear what he tried to do, they'll keep him longer than that."

"They'll send him to jail probably."

"I hope so," said Hugh. "Any man who would try to blow up a bridge and kill crowds of people deserves worse than jail."

"They'll give him five or ten years all right," said Bob.

"Yes, and when they try his case we'll have to act as witnesses I suppose."

"I wouldn't mind that," Bob exclaimed. "It might be a lot of fun."

"Aren't these plotters silly?" said Hugh. "They may be

able to blow up a plant or a bridge here and there, but they'll lose more than they gain."

"Why so?"

"Because it'll make the people mad. When they once get angry they'll fight and work much harder to defeat Germany. Half the people in this country don't seem to realize that we are at war now, but when a few of them get blown up we'll begin to do something."

They discussed the war and the possibility of sending American troops to France. Hugh wanted to go into the aviation corps when he was old enough but Bob thought the infantry and solid ground under his feet would be good enough for him.

Presently they came near home. Hugh lived two blocks farther down the street than Bob and consequently he had to pass the Cooks' house on his way.

"There's the Wernbergs'," said Bob. "A light in the second story back window, and two automobiles in front."

"Do you suppose they're up to anything?" exclaimed Hugh.

"I suspect them all right, but how can we prove it?"

"I have an idea," Hugh exclaimed suddenly. The two boys were standing on the opposite side of the street from the Wernbergs' house, regarding it curiously.

"What is it?"

Paul G. Tomlinson

"Can you get your automobile?"

"I guess so, if Heinrich hasn't taken the family out."

"Let's get it and follow one of those machines. In that way we can see where the people live who are at the Wernbergs'. Maybe we can learn something about them if we know who they are."

"A good scheme," exclaimed Bob readily. "We'll have to be awfully careful though; if they ever found out we were following them it might go hard with us."

"We'll be careful all right," said Hugh grimly. "Come ahead, we want to be ready to start and they may leave at any time."

The two boys walked quickly up the street, taking care to keep on the opposite side from the Wernberg home. When they arrived in front of the Cooks' they darted across the street and hurried along the driveway until they came to the garage. The door was shut and locked. Bob knocked loudly.

There was no reply. Bob looked at his watch under the light of a match which Hugh struck. It was twenty minutes of eleven.

"That's queer," he muttered. "Heinie is usually in bed long before this."

"Maybe he is now, and is asleep," Hugh suggested.

Bob glanced up at the second story window. "I don't think so," he said. "The window is closed in the room where he usually sleeps, and I know he is a crank on fresh air."

"Throw some gravel at it," said Hugh. "That'll get him up if he's there."

This plan was followed, but with no success.

"He's out," said Bob finally. "What'll we do?"

"Is the car there?"

"Yes, but what good will it do us if we can't get in?"

"Haven't you got a key to the garage up at the house?"

"Father has one, but I don't dare wake him now." Bob glanced at the house and the absence of lights on the first and second floors convinced him that his family were all in bed. A single light shone from a window on the third floor where Lena, the cook, slept.

"Maybe we can force a window," suggested Hugh. "You can open the door from the inside, can't you?"

"Oh, yes," said Bob. "Let's try a window anyway."

They went around the corner of the garage and the first window they tried yielded immediately. A moment later both boys had clambered inside, and presently Bob found the electric light button. As the light flooded the garage Heinrich's angora cat rose sleepily from the tonneau of the automobile and stretched himself. A cloth covering over the parrot's cage kept that garrulous bird quiet. Percy lay stretched out in the water which filled his tub.

"The dog must be out with Heinrich," said Bob.

He seated himself in the driver's seat of the car, and Hugh lifted the drowsy cat to the floor. Bob pushed a button, put his foot on the self-starter and the engine started. Heinrich always backed the car into the garage so that it was headed in the right direction as it stood. Hugh undid the spring catch on the door and rolled the door back. They were now ready to start.

"I'll go down by the street and watch the Wernbergs," said Hugh. "I hope they haven't gotten away while we have been fooling around here."

"I guess not," said Bob. "When they start you whistle twice and I'll be with you right away."

"All right," agreed Hugh. "You'd better run with your lights dimmed."

"I shall, don't worry."

Hugh hurried away. Bob was left alone in the car and he presently shut off the engine. He had wished to warm up the motor so that it would start readily when the time came; he was convinced that it would do so now.

He thought over the events of the day, and for the first time he realized that he was tired. Excitement had spurred him on and the intense interest he took in the war had made him forget all else. He wondered if he and Hugh were starting off on a wild goose chase now. What particular reason had they to suspect the Wernbergs anyway? True, all Germans were more or less under suspicion just then, but why the Wernbergs any more than the others? He recalled his fight with Frank that morning, and his father's remarks. Perhaps it was just as well to go out that night after all.

Bob thought of the war and the terrible things the Germans had done. What brutes and beasts they were! The Germans had been busy in the United States too. The big factory at Eddystone had been blown up that day, with the loss of a hundred and twenty-five lives, mostly of girls. That showed what the American people had to guard against.

"I hate them all!" muttered Bob angrily. He took that back a moment later, however, as he thought of Heinrich. Surely their chauffeur was as faithful and kindly a soul as ever lived; his love for animals proved that. Then there was Lena, their cook, a buxom woman of forty who had never been heard to utter a cross word in her life.

Heinrich was capable of getting mad, however, particularly about the car. Bob wondered what he would say if he should arrive home now, and find him preparing to go out in it and perhaps get it dirty.

His reverie was suddenly interrupted by the sound of two whistles. A moment later the motor was purring softly, and with the headlights dimmed, the big sixty horse-power car slid out of the garage and started silently down the driveway.

CHAPTER VII

IN THE NIGHT

"They're starting," said Hugh in a low voice. He jumped upon the running board as Bob came along, and climbed into the front seat beside him. "Let's wait here a minute," he whispered.

Down the street in front of the Wernbergs' house they could see men getting into the two automobiles. Presently the whirr of the motors came to their ears and the two cars started. One came towards them and the other went in the opposite direction.

"Which one shall we follow?" whispered Bob.

"Let's follow the one going the other way."

They rolled out of the driveway and started down the street. As they turned into the avenue the first car passed them, a gray roadster bespeaking power and speed in its every detail. Two men were seated in it. Bob and Hugh obtained a fleeting glimpse of them as they flashed by. The tail light of the car they intended to follow showed a dim, red spot far down the street.

"Speed her up a little, Bob," urged Hugh. "We don't want to lose them."

"We can't keep too close to them either," said Bob. "Besides, my thumb and forefinger are pretty sore from that fuse burn and it's hard to grip the wheel."

"Mine are sore too," said Hugh. "Put on gloves."

"I haven't any with me."

"I have; take mine."

Still watching the small red dot ahead of them Bob managed to slip on Hugh's right-hand glove. It was a great help to him in driving.

"They've turned a corner," exclaimed Hugh suddenly. "Faster, Bob!"

Bob pressed his foot on the accelerator and the car leaped forward as if it were a living thing. A moment later they reached the cross street and turned into it, peering anxiously ahead. The car they were following was still in sight.

"Keep about two hundred yards in back of them," Hugh advised.

"We mustn't lose them."

"No, and we don't want them to get suspicious either."

"They're turning another corner," exclaimed Bob after a few moments.

"Speed it up now that they can't see us."

Bob did so and they ame to the corner just in time to

see the car they were following pull up at the curb in front of a white stucco house.

"Go ahead, Bob! Go ahead!" urged Hugh. "Don't turn!"

Bob kept straight on. "What street was that?" he asked.

"Elm Street."

"Isn't that where the German on the bridge told Harold he lived?"

"Why so it is," exclaimed Hugh.

"I wonder what number that house is."

"I don't know. Let's see, Howard Seeley lives on Elm Street, just the next block down; his number is eleven hundred and something."

"The German told Harold he lived at twelve eighty-two, and I'll bet you that was the house."

"Whew!" whistled Hugh. "I wonder if it was."

"They probably went to find out why the bridge wasn't blown up to-night," said Bob. "Do you suppose that could be it?"

"Maybe. We could have told them quicker if they'd come to us though," chuckled Hugh. "They'll probably give that fellow the mischief for failing."

"They can't get at him if he's in jail."

"That's so. Suppose we're called as witnesses at his

trial? They'll learn that we spoiled their game and our lives won't be worth two cents."

"Well, if those men are plotters we must prove it before the case even comes to trial."

"Do you suppose they have a regular organization to blow up everything around here that they can?" said Hugh. "I should think the secret service would get after them."

"Probably it has; no doubt the names of all those men are listed."

"That is, if they really are plotters."

"Of course. Where are you going!"

They had kept straight on down the road and were now on the outskirts of the city. The houses were fewer and more scattered all the time and presently the boys would be in the open country.

"I don't know," said Bob. "I was just going ahead without thinking."

"We'd better go back, hadn't we? We must be about three miles from home."

"There's a road up ahead here to the right," said Bob. "We can turn down there and go back that way."

When they were about two hundred yards distant from the road in question, an automobile came out of it and turned into the main highway. A moment later it was speeding along in front of Bob and Hugh, the roar of its cutout coming faintly to their ears.

"Bob," exclaimed Hugh excitedly, "that's the gray roadster!"

"What gray roadster?"

"The one we passed in front of your house. It came from the Wernbergs'."

"Shall we follow it?"

"Certainly. It's going like the wind though."

"Well, it can't lose us," said Bob grimly. He advanced the spark, gave the motor more gas and they were soon tearing through the night at fifty miles an hour. Over the crest of a hill in front of them, the gray roadster was outlined for a moment and then disappeared.

Up the grade of the hill Bob drove the big car. When they arrived at the top they peered ahead anxiously for any sign of the machine they followed. Nothing was to be seen of it.

"It's gone," exclaimed Hugh.

"Perhaps not," said Bob. "It can't be very far ahead of us anyway."

They continued down the road at breakneck speed, passing through a clump of woods that lined both sides. Bob forced the motor to its utmost, but no sign of the gray roadster could they discover. Finally he brought the car to a dead stop and turned to Hugh.

"What became of that car?" he demanded. "They weren't far enough ahead of us to have gotten out of sight so quickly."

"They must have turned off into another road," said Hugh. "I don't see what else could have happened."

"But there are no roads into which they could have turned."

"Are you sure?"

"Positively."

Both boys relapsed into silence, completely mystified by the strangeness of the thing. Apparently the roadster had vanished from the face of the earth.

"Wait a minute," cried Bob suddenly. "There is a road back there too."

"I thought there must be."

"Remember those woods back there, just this side of the hill?"

"Yes. That's where we used to go for chestnuts in the fall."

"That's the place. Remember the old house back in there?"

"It's deserted and tumble-down."

"I know it, but there's an old wagon road leading to it."

"Do you think that is where they went?" exclaimed Hugh in surprise.

"Where else could they have gone?"

"I don't know, I'm sure."

"Shall we go back there and see?"

"We can't run the car in there."

"Why not? We can if they can."

"Suppose we should meet them coming out?"

"That's right," exclaimed Bob. "I tell you what we can do though. We'll run back down the road and leave the car and then go to the old house on foot."

"Good scheme," said Hugh readily. "We can hide the car somewhere I suppose."

"Oh, yes. We'll leave it a little way off the road under some trees."

A few moments later Bob had turned the car around and they were speeding back in the direction whence they had come.

"You know where the road is, don't you?" asked Hugh.

"I do," said Bob confidently. "We'll leave the car about a quarter of a mile this side of it and then walk."

"I wonder if they could have gone to that old deserted house," mused Hugh.

"Maybe. I swear I don't see why though."

"We're probably chasing moonbeams," said Hugh.

"Perhaps we are, but we're having a lot of fun anyway."

"Of course we are," exclaimed Hugh, "and I'm for going ahead."

A moment later Bob slowed down the car. A clump of trees appeared alongside the road, and shifting into second speed Bob carefully steered his course toward them. In the shadow of the trees he stopped, shut off the motor, turned off the lights, and stepped out. Hugh got out on the other side.

"Here we are," whispered Bob. "I guess it's all right to leave the car here."

"I should think so," Hugh agreed. "We're about fifteen yards from the road and I don't believe any one would notice it in here."

They started down the road, keeping well to one side, so that they would not show up against the faint white ribbon of the highway as it stretched through the country. After a walk of about five minutes Bob halted.

"There's the road," he whispered, pointing ahead.

"Come on then," urged Hugh. "Carefully now."

It was a weird sensation to be stealing along in the darkness, and the hearts of both boys were pounding. They turned from the main road and started down the narrow wagon track through the woods. It was much darker there and difficult to pick one's path.

A dry twig snapped under Hugh's foot and the boys stopped short, their breath coming fast. The hoot of an owl directly overhead startled them violently and unconsciously they clutched each other's arm. The giant trees loomed black and forbidding in the darkness, and it was easy to imagine all kinds of things lurking behind to spring out at them.

"I don't like this," whispered Hugh. "How far is it from here?"

"Just a short distance. I don't like it either."

Presently Bob tugged at Hugh's sleeve. "There's a light," he said softly.

A faint glimmer appeared through the darkness ahead. Presently the boys were able to see that it came from a lantern held by some man standing in the open doorway of the old house. A moment later four others appeared from within and came out to the tumble-down porch. Bob and Hugh looked on with bated breath. What could it all mean?

CHAPTER VIII

A STRANGE OCCURRENCE

The man with the lantern advanced to the edge of the porch, holding the lantern at arm's length and shoulder high. In the flickering light Bob and Hugh could see the others putting on their overcoats. Presently there was a flash of light as the powerful searchlights of an automobile were turned on; only for a second or two, however, as they were quickly extinguished.

"There's the gray roadster," whispered Hugh.

The two boys were crouched behind a fallen tree, an obstruction they had been on the point of climbing when they had spied the lantern. They could hear the men walking about near the house, and frequently could even catch the sound of voices.

Presently they heard the whirr of a motor. Dimmed lights were turned on in the roadster and soon it started.

"Lie low," whispered Hugh. "They mustn't see us."

Bob needed no cautioning on that score, however.

The car rumbled toward them as if it were feeling its

way. The wagon-road was some ten yards to the left of the spot where the two boys were concealed. Directly to it the roadster went, its two glowing eyes giving it the appearance of some gigantic bug. With bated breath Hugh and Bob watched its progress. Presently it passed them and lumbered away over the rough road.

"How many men were in it?" whispered Hugh.

"Three, I think."

"There were only two when we passed it in front of your house."

"I know it. There must be a couple more men here, too."

"Ssh," hissed Hugh softly, grasping his companion by the wrist.

Voices could be heard, coming nearer and nearer to their hiding place. Once again the two boys almost stopped breathing while they waited for the speakers to pass. They could make out two shadowy forms following the same course taken by the automobile. The two men conversed earnestly together in tones so low, that the listeners could not overhear what was said. After a few moments the sound of the voices died away and Hugh and Bob were left alone. That is, they were alone as far as they could tell.

"Well," said Hugh finally. "They're gone."

"Seems so," admitted Bob. "We can't be sure though."

"Were those men talking German?"

"I couldn't tell."

"Neither could I for sure, but I thought they were."

"Probably so," said Bob. "At any rate it looks to me as if there was some queer business going on in this place."

"It certainly does. I wonder what's in that house?"

"Shall we go and see?"

"You don't catch me in that house at this time of night," said Hugh grimly.

"How about coming out here to-morrow, then?"

"To-morrow's Saturday, isn't it?"

"Yes."

"All right," said Hugh. "I'll come out with you."

"And now we'd better go home."

"I guess we had. It must be nearly midnight."

They arose from their cramped positions on the ground and stealthily began to retrace their steps. They were even more wary on their way out than they had been going in, for they could not be sure that they would not meet some of the men they had seen about the old house. Just before they came to the end of the wagon-road they heard the sound of a motor and saw the lights of an automobile speeding down the main road in the direction of High Ridge.

"Sounds like our car," said Bob. "All those motors make the same sort of noise."

"Pretty good ears you have," remarked Hugh.

"You ought to see old Heinie," said Bob. "He may look stupid, but he can tell almost any make of car just by the noise it makes."

"What'll he say when you get home?" queried Hugh.

"He'll be mad. He doesn't think I know how to drive the car, and if there is any dirt on it he'll be madder yet."

"The roads aren't muddy now though."

"I know it, but he'll be cross if there's dust on it even."

They emerged on the main road, looked carefully in both directions, and then still keeping to the side of the road, started back toward the spot where they had left the car. A ghostly moon, in its last quarter, shed its pale light on the highway, and aided the boys to distinguish their surroundings.

"There's the place," said Bob a moment later.

They ran quickly across the road and hurried towards the clump of trees where they had hidden the car. Both boys would feel relieved when they were seated in their conveyance once more, and on their way home. It was nervous work prowling around the countryside at night with a suspicious gang of men lurking near.

Bob and Hugh hurried along side by side and presently

came to the patch of trees, which was their destination. A feeling of relief came over them that soon they would be speeding back to High Ridge.

Suddenly Bob uttered an exclamation of surprise and stopped short.

"The car is gone," he gasped.

CHAPTER IX

ANOTHER SURPRISE

At first the two boys were too amazed to speak. They stared blankly at the spot where the car had been concealed. It now was nowhere to be seen.

"Is this the place?" exclaimed Hugh, the first to regain his senses.

"I know it is," said Bob. "I ran the car right up under that big birch tree so that I could surely mark the spot."

"Well!" gasped Hugh, unable to say more.

"What'll we do?" Bob almost sobbed. "Some one has stolen the car, and it is all my fault. What will father say?"

"You'll have to tell him the circumstances," said Hugh lamely. "I don't know what else you can do."

"But the car is gone," insisted Bob, his mind unable to grasp any idea beyond that. "The car is gone."

"Maybe it'll come back," said Hugh. "Stolen cars are often recovered."

He lighted a match and held it close to the ground. There were the marks made by the tires in the damp earth. There was no doubt that this was the place.

"Who could have taken it?" demanded Bob.

Both boys were silent and the same thought flashed through their minds at once.

"One of those men from that old house," said Hugh.

"They must have had sentries posted," said Bob and he glanced about him nervously. "Probable they watched us leave it here and when we went back into the woods they took it. Probably they followed us and watched us all the time too; very likely they're watching us now."

"Let's go home," exclaimed Hugh. "I've had enough of this."

"But the car," protested Bob.

"It's gone, isn't it?" said Hugh. "We can't find it by just standing around here. The best thing we can do is to hurry back to High Ridge as fast as we can and report it to police headquarters."

"It's over three miles," said Bob.

"Suppose it is," Hugh exclaimed. "Suppose it was twenty miles: we'd have to go just the same. We may get a lift on the way."

"Not at this time of night."

"Anyway we'd better start; we may be in danger here."

This latter consideration had great weight with Bob. He realized that enemies of one kind or another were there, or had been recently, in that neighborhood and he had no desire to meet them, unarmed as he was. His judgment also told him that Hugh's suggestion about reporting the loss of the car to the police was the only feasible one under the circumstances.

"Come on," he urged. "Let's go home."

"Some one may come along and offer us a ride," said Hugh hopefully.

"I'm afraid there won't be many people out at this time of night," returned Bob disconsolately. "I wish I knew what had happened to the car."

They proceeded in silence, glancing about them nervously for fear that they might be the victims of some further surprise. For a half-mile they kept to the side of the road, for little as they cared to walk where the darkness was thickest, they knew they would not be as exposed there as they would be in the middle of the road. When they reached the top of the hill, however, they became bolder and ventured out upon the paved highway.

They walked swiftly, every few yards one or the other of the boys turning to glance behind them to see if they were followed. The night was clear, and the stars were shining brilliantly; hardly a breath of air was stirring. Presently they came within sight of the town, and the sound of the clock on the town hall striking one came faintly to their ears.

"Whew," said Bob, "it's late."

"I should say so," Hugh agreed, "and I was just thinking of everything we have done to-day. We've certainly been busy."

"We may be even busier to-morrow."

"Why so?"

"Well, if we go back to that house again, you can't tell what we'll get into."

"I wonder if we ought to report to the police what we've seen."

"Probably we should," said Bob. "I'd like to go it alone though."

"And so should I. Let's wait a day or two longer anyway."

"I hope it won't be too late then."

"We'll risk it anyway," said Hugh. "Look, here comes an automobile."

"It's going the wrong way for us. Get over on the side of the road."

In the distance appeared the headlights of an automobile rapidly approaching. The two boys hurried to one side of the road and took up their positions behind the shelter of some low growing bushes. The car was traveling fast and as it neared the spot where they were concealed they could hear the thunder of the cutout. A moment later it roared past them and disappeared.

"Hugh," exclaimed Bob. "The gray roadster!"

"It was for sure!" said Hugh. "What do you think of that?"

"It was going back to the old house probably."

"I guess it was. Perhaps after all, we should report to the police."

"Wait till after to-morrow," said Bob. "We'll go out in the morning and take a look around there on our own account."

"We may have to spend to-morrow looking for your car."

"That's true, but let's wait and see what happens anyway."

They continued on their way homeward and soon came within the outskirts of the town. The houses were darkened and apparently every one was in bed and asleep. The sound of the boys' footsteps on the pavements echoed loudly along the still, deserted streets.

"Here's Elm Street," said Hugh. "Let's turn down here; it's on our way home and we can pass right by that stucco house."

"All right," Bob agreed, and they turned the corner.

"That's the place," whispered Hugh a few moments later.

"There's a light in the third story," said Bob in a

low tone.

"Perhaps they're waiting up for that German bomb planter," chuckled Hugh. "I guess he won't be home to-night."

"Don't joke about it, Hugh. I feel sorry for the man's family."

"So do I, but I don't feel sorry for him."

"I should say not! Anything they do to him won't be half bad enough."

"The snake," muttered Hugh. "I'd like to have one look inside that room up there though and see what is going on." He glanced up at the lighted window questioningly. As he did so the shade was thrown up and the window opened by some man who thrust his head out and looked around. Bob and Hugh shrank back within the shadow of a nearby tree. They caught only a fleeting glimpse of the man's face, and saw that it was no one they knew. He had closely cropped hair and a bristling mustache turned up at the ends.

"Who do you suppose that was?" whispered Bob a moment later, as the man they watched withdrew his head and shut the window.

"Never saw him before," said Hugh.

"He looked like a German though. Let's get home before he comes outside and begins to prowl around."

Walking on the ground so that they would not make any noise they hurried on. A few moments later they stood in front of the Cooks' house.

"There's a light in your house too," said Hugh. "This and that house on Elm Street are the only ones where people seem to be awake."

"That's Lena's room," said Bob.

"The cook?"

"Yes."

"She's a German, isn't she?"

"Look here, Hugh," laughed Bob. "You can't make me suspicious about Lena. She has been our cook ever since I was born. She's the most faithful and kind-hearted woman that ever lived. Why she's practically one of the family."

"Then what is she doing up there all this time?" demanded Hugh. "Her room was lighted up when we started out."

"I don't know what she's doing," said Bob. "Reading, maybe. You can't get me excited about her, and just because some Germans are disloyal you mustn't think they all are."

"All right," said Hugh. "I'd watch them all though."

"You're crazy," said Bob. "What I want to know is what happened to our automobile. Tomorrow morning before breakfast you'll see me on my way to police headquarters to report it. Heinie was going to fix the puncture in my bicycle to-day and I'll go down on that."

"Will you telephone to me about eight o'clock?"

"I will," said Bob, "and if there's nothing we can do about the automobile well take our bicycles and ride out to the old deserted house."

"Good, and now we'd better sneak to bed, for we shan't get much sleep as it is."

"All right. Good night."

"Good night," said Hugh and turned off down the street.

Bob made his way quietly across the lawn towards the house, glancing up curiously once or twice at the lighted window in Lena's room. As he looked the light went out. "Poor old Hugh," he thought. "How silly he is to be suspicious of Lena." He tiptoed up the steps and across the porch, let himself in carefully with his latch key, and stole upstairs.

He wished to get into bed without waking any of the family, and was successful in this, for soon he was snugly under the covers without having disturbed any one. It was a long time before sleep came to him, however. He was greatly worried about the loss of the car and he dreaded having to tell his father about it the next day. Of course his father would understand, but no one could be blamed for being upset at the loss of a new automobile, particularly as the result of what might prove to be a wild goose chase.

Heinrich too would be furious, and Bob expected their

chauffeur to knock on his door at any moment and demand where the automobile was. Heinrich did not go to bed until the car was safely in the garage, and as a rule he washed it no matter how late the hour was.

Bob's black eye throbbed somewhat too, his fingers smarted from the burn of the lighted fuse, and his brain was reeling with the events of the day. At length, however, he fell asleep and strange to say he slept dreamlessly. He had taken care to set his alarm-clock for half-past six and it seemed to him that his eyes had been closed only a very few minutes when it went off close beside his ear. He clutched it quickly and stifled the alarm so as not to awaken the rest of the household; a moment later he had jumped out of bed and was getting into his clothes.

He glanced out of the window and saw that it was light outside. The early morning sun shone on the bare limbs of the trees and made them glisten. Here and there a bud could be seen almost ready to burst its shell and Bob rejoiced to see signs of the coming of spring and summer. He was not happy, however, for the loss of the car weighed him down and oppressed him. Even the awakening beauties of nature did not cheer him up and that was unusual in Bob's case.

A few moments later he was fully dressed except for his shoes. He held them in one hand, and in his stocking feet slipped out of his room and stole downstairs. He opened the front door carefully and then sat down on the steps to put on his shoes. As he busied himself a bicycle passed along the street in front of the house, and Bob recognized the rider as Frank Wernberg.

"What's he doing out at this time of day?" muttered Bob angrily. He sat motionless and as Frank did not look toward the house he decided that he had not been seen. Bob yawned, rubbed his eyes sleepily, and stretched. He suddenly recalled the loss of the automobile, and jumping to his feet started toward the garage.

As he came near he saw that the front door of the garage was open. That was queer, he thought, as Heinrich never left it open at night. Then he recalled that he and Hugh had left it open the night before and that probably Heinrich had left it undisturbed so that they could run in the car without trouble when they returned. Heinrich had no doubt come in and gone to sleep, and had not yet discovered that the car was missing.

Imagine Bob's surprise therefore when he turned the corner of the building and saw the car standing in its accustomed place. Heinrich was washing it as if nothing in the world had happened.

CHAPTER X

BOB IS MYSTIFIED

Bob stopped and stared in amazement. He could scarcely believe his eyes. There was the car that had disappeared so mysteriously the night before, in its right place, and undamaged as far as he could see.

"Heinrich," he exclaimed in amazement.

The chauffeur, a hose in one hand, a big sponge in the other, and wearing high rubber boots, looked up inquiringly.

"What are you doing up so early?" he asked.

"Where did the car come from?" demanded Bob.

Heinrich straightened up and gazed at Bob.

"What you mean?" he inquired.

"Who brought the car home?"

"How do I know? Maybe your father use it last night. Whoever do it, get it all covered mit dust."

"But," stammered Bob, "the car was stolen."

"What!" exclaimed Heinrich. "What you talking about?"

"What time did you get in last night?" Bob inquired, becoming more and more anxious and bewildered every moment.

"Twelve o'clock," said Heinrich. "What you mean the car iss stolen?"

"Was it here when you came home?"

"Certainly it was here. What you talking about?"

"I don't know," said Bob weakly, and he sat down on the running board and passed his hand across his brow.

"Are you sick?" asked Heinrich anxiously. "You look pale."

"I'm not sick," said Bob. "I guess I'm crazy," and he held his head in both hands, staring blankly at the floor.

Heinrich did not know what to make of the strange behavior of his employer's son. He stared at him curiously, and it was plain to see that he was telling the truth in all he said.

"What you mean the car iss stolen?" he inquired finally.

"Nothing," said Bob blankly. "It's too much for me."

"I go to a party last night," said Heinrich. "I come home late and the door here iss open. Here iss the car too. Why you think it stolen?"

"I don't know," said Bob. "I guess I must have dreamt it."

"You are sick," exclaimed Heinrich. "You had better go back and go to bed. If you wish I go with you to the house."

"No," said Bob. "I'm all right." He rose to his feet dazedly, looked in bewilderment at the car again and started out.

"I have a loss," said Heinrich, convinced that Bob was probably all right.

"What's that?" demanded Bob, turning around.

"Burglars," said Heinrich.

"Where? In the garage here?"

"Yes. Last night," and Heinrich brushed a tear from his eye.

"You did?" exclaimed Bob. "They didn't steal all that money you had yesterday, did they?"

"No," said Heinrich sorrowfully. "I almost wish they had. They steal Percy."

"Percy," cried Bob, greatly relieved. "Why should any one steal him?"

"I do not know. I come down this morning and I look in the tub to say good-morning to Percy. The tub iss here, but Percy iss gone."

"There are some queer things going on around here, Heinie," said Bob.

"I like to catch the man what steal him," said Heinrich fiercely.

"I'd like to catch lots of people," said Bob. "Maybe he fell out of the tub."

"He could not do that," exclaimed Heinrich. "The sides iss too high."

"Well, it's certainly strange." Bob went out of the garage and started slowly back toward the house. Heinrich, sorrowing over the loss of his alligator, with a sigh took up the sponge and hose again and fell to washing the car once more.

Bob returned to his room, washed his face and hands, something he had neglected to do before, and went downstairs again. He glanced at the morning newspaper, full of war news and preparations for war; one column told of the arrest of many Germans all over the country, men who were suspected of caring more for the Fatherland than they did for the United States.

There was no mention of the bomb episode on the railroad bridge the night before, however. Bob knew that the authorities would not permit the publication of any such items if they could prevent it so he was not surprised. Presently the rest of the family appeared and they went in to breakfast.

Mr. Cook's mail was lying on the table by his plate; it

as his custom every morning to glance it over while he was eating. While Mrs. Cook talked to Bob about Harold, her husband looked through his letters. Suddenly he uttered an exclamation of surprise. "Here's a queer thing," he said.

"What?" demanded Mrs. Cook anxiously. She had been very nervous lately.

"This postcard," said Mr. Cook. "Listen to what it says. 'Take the advice of one who knows and keep your automobile home at night.'"

Bob turned pale. "What does it mean!" inquired Mrs. Cook.

"I'm sure I don't know," said her husband.

"How is it signed?"

"It is not signed at all."

"I can't imagine what it's all about," said Mr. Cook. "As far as I know, our car hasn't been out of the garage at night for over a week."

"Perhaps Heinrich has had it out," Mrs. Cook suggested.

"I'll ask him right after breakfast," said Mr. Cook. "They must have mistaken our car for some one else's."

"Who do you suppose sent it?"

"I'm sure I don't know," said her husband musingly.

"At any rate I think I shall turn it over to the police; I don't like the look of it."

Throughout this conversation Bob sat silent. He thought perhaps he could explain part of the mystery to his father, but he was puzzled as to whether he ought to do so or not. On the other hand if his father called in the police, he knew that he and Hugh would have small chance of clearing up the matter themselves.

"It worries me so, Robert," exclaimed Mrs. Cook. "I am so afraid that something will happen to you, especially as you are making war supplies at the factory now."

"The plant is guarded," said her husband. "Besides I think I owe it to my country to help all I can, don't you?"

"Of course, but suppose some of your guards are treacherous."

"They are all trusted employees of American birth."

"No Germans at all?"

"The man in charge at night has parents born in Germany; you know him, Karl Hoffmann, the one who wants to marry Lena. He is just as faithful and true as she is. I can vouch for all the others as well."

"He's all right I guess," said Mrs. Cook with a smile. "Even if Heinrich doesn't like him." Heinrich and Karl Hoffmann were rivals for Lena's affections, and they despised each other. Lena, however, seemed to like them both equally well, or at least she did not care enough about either to marry him.

Bob used to delight in teasing Heinrich about his rival. When Karl was on the premises Heinrich would sulk in the garage and mutter threats against him. Karl was twice Heinrich's size, but the little blue-eyed, spectacled chauffeur never seemed to question his ability to deal with him.

Mr. Cook rose from the table. "I'll go down and ask Heinrich about this car business," he said, "and then I'll go down to the office." He kissed Mrs. Cook and Louise and left the room. Bob followed him out. His father put on his coat and hat and stepped out onto the front porch. A sudden resolution seized Bob.

"Father," he said.

"What is it, Bob?" asked Mr. Cook, turning to glance at his son.

"I think I can explain about the car."

"You can?" exclaimed his father in surprise, looking curiously at Bob's pale face.

"Yes, sir," said Bob, nervously. "It's a sort of a long story. Shall I tell it all?"

"Certainly. Come out here to the summer house."

They walked in silence to the little rustic house on the lawn and sat down side by side on the rough wooden seat. Bob was excited, but still determined that the best thing for him to do was to tell his father the whole story. He knew his father would understand and see things from his point of view; they were more like two brothers than a father and son.

"Hugh and I had the car out last night," said Bob, and then he began at the beginning and related the entire story through to the end. He told of their visit to the armory, their meeting with Harold on the bridge, the narrow escape with the bomb, their decision to watch the Wernbergs' house, their trip to the deserted house, the disappearance of the automobile, and finally its strange return.

Mr. Cook listened intently throughout the whole narrative, one exclamation as Bob told of the bomb episode being his sole interruption.

"That card must have been sent by the one that brought the car back," said Bob.

"It would seem so," his father agreed, and fell silent, thinking.

"That was a close call you boys had with that bomb," he said finally.

"Yes, sir," said Bob.

"What have you planned to do to-day?"

"We were going to report the loss of the car to police headquarters and then go out to the deserted house again, to see what we could find."

"You weren't going to say anything to the police about it?"

"No, sir."

"That might be dangerous, you know."

"Yes, sir," said Bob. "We wanted to solve the thing ourselves if we could though."

"I don't know about that," said Mr. Cook musingly. "I hate to think of you two boys fooling around out there with a lot of desperate men around."

"Don't do anything until this afternoon anyway," Bob pleaded.

Mr. Cook thought for a minute. "All right," he agreed. "Ill wait until after luncheon. Do you and Hugh expect to go out there this morning?"

"Yes, sir."

"Have you got a gun?"

"No, we haven't."

"Well, there's an automatic pistol and two boxes of cartridges in the second drawer of my bureau. Go up and get them before you start, for I think you ought to be armed. And above all don't say anything about it to your mother."

"Certainly not," exclaimed Bob, much excited that his father was helping them.

"Be careful," warned his father. "I'll be home for luncheon and we'll talk more then."

Heinrich appeared with the car and Mr. Cook got in and was soon on the way to his office. Bob hurried into the house to telephone to Hugh and possess himself of his father's automatic pistol.

Hugh promised to hurry over as fast as he could, and he could tell from the tone of Bob's voice that something stirring was on foot. Bob had answered his question about the car evasively and he was anxious to hear the latest developments. Consequently by the time that Bob had tucked the pistol safely in his back pocket and had gone to the garage for his bicycle, Hugh appeared.

Bob related the story of the car and its strange return, and also told about the postal card his father had received that morning. The mystery seemed to deepen rather than clear up, and both boys were profoundly mystified by the strange events of the previous day.

"Your eye's better anyway," remarked Hugh.

"Yes," said Bob. "But I may get another one to-day."

"We'll hope not. When do you want to start?"

"Right away."

"Come ahead then," and jumping on their bicycles the two boys pedalled out of the yard. Little did they dream that bright April morning, as they rode along, that they were headed for adventures which would make the events that had gone before appear mild in comparison.

CHAPTER XI

THE DESERTED HOUSE

"Somebody stole Percy," said Bob when they had ridden a little way.

"The alligator?"

"Yes. Heinrich's pet, you know."

"Why should any one want to do that?"

"I can't imagine, and poor old Heinie is all broken up about it. I've never seen any one who liked animals as much as he does."

"Who do you suppose did it?"

"I've no idea. Perhaps the man who returned the car stole him and is planning to wait until he grows big and then train him to come and bite us," laughed Bob.

"Let's hope not," smiled Hugh. "There are too many strange things going on for me to understand just now. My brain is all mixed up."

"And so's mine. I should like to know who sent that postal card though."

"Perhaps we'll get on the trail of it when we get to the deserted house."

"Do you suppose we can break in?"

"Perhaps we can. I've brought an electric flashlight along that may come in handy."

"A good idea," exclaimed Bob. "I have an idea myself."

"What's that?"

"We'd better not ride too far down the road. Let's leave our wheels this side of the hill, and then go across the country and come in to the house from the back. In that way I think we'll stand less chance of being seen."

"Probably you're right. At any rate I hope no one steals our bicycles."

"I wonder if they'd be returned," said Bob. "Wasn't that a queer thing?"

"It certainly was."

They rode in silence for some time and presently came within sight of the hill of which they had been speaking. They dismounted from their bicycles, and wheeling them by their sides started across the fields. A hundred yards from the main road they concealed them under a clump of bushes and then continued on their way. They walked for about a half-mile until they saw the fringe of the woods in the middle of which stood the deserted house.

Paul G. Tomlinson

"Bob," said Hugh suddenly. "I know who took your automobile."

"What?" exclaimed Bob. "What are you talking about?"

"I know who took your automobile."

"Who!"

"Heinrich."

Bob burst out laughing. "What are you talking about?" he demanded. "How could Heinrich take it? Hugh, you're going crazy."

"Isn't Heinrich a German?"

"He is."

"Weren't there a lot of Germans meeting out here in the old house last night?"

"We think so. I still don't see what that has to do with Heinie."

"How do you know Heinrich wasn't here?" asked Hugh.

"You mean that Heinrich is a plotter?" exclaimed Bob, suddenly realizing what his friend was driving at.

"He might bear watching," said Hugh. "He and that German cook of yours."

"They're both honest and reliable," exclaimed Bob warmly.

"Well," said Hugh, "I heard a story last night about two men coming to a house where they had a nice 'honest and reliable' German girl and demanding to see her. The owner of the house refused, and the men then showed secret service badges. Of course when he saw the badges he had to do as they said and he called in the girl. As soon as she came into the room one of the men went up to her and grabbed hold of her hair. Well, sir, it came right off her head and then they discovered that the maid was nothing more nor less than a man, a German in disguise, trying to get information for his government."

"Is that a true story?" exclaimed Bob in amazement.

"The man in whose house it happened told it to father," said Hugh. "It only goes to show that you can't be too careful. I wouldn't be too sure about Heinrich and Lena if I were you. The Germans are a bad lot and I suspect them all."

"Perhaps," said Bob. "Still Heinie and Lena are different."

"They may be tools of Mr. Wernberg for all you know."

"You're foolish," exclaimed Bob. "Why even if they weren't loyal to the United States they'd be loyal to father and mother. I know that."

Hugh shrugged his shoulders. "It sounds fishy to me, that's all," he said. "Didn't Heinrich say he went to a

Paul G. Tomlinson

party last night? How do you know the party wasn't held out here, and that he just happened to run across your car and decided to bring it home."

"If he had he would have washed the car last night, not this morning."

"Why so?"

"Because he's so methodical, like all the Germans. He never could have slept if he had known the car was dirty."

"Why, Bob," Hugh protested, "Heinrich says he didn't come in until twelve o'clock and he says the car was there then. Why didn't he notice that it was dirty then? I'd like to know."

"He probably didn't light but one light in the garage and didn't notice it."

"Sounds likely," snorted Hugh. "Take my advice and watch 'em both."

"They're just as faithful as you or I," exclaimed Bob. "You can't talk me into getting suspicious of those two."

"The faithful ones are the ones to suspect," said Hugh grimly.

"Nonsense," said Bob, but his friend's words nevertheless set him to thinking. What if Heinrich and Lena should turn out to be working in the interests of Germany? He recalled the light in Lena's room the night before, and then he thought of all the money

Heinrich had had and how embarrassed and uneasy he had been when Bob spoke of it. Ugly stories of Germans crowded through his mind, but he refused to believe that their two servants were of that sort.

Presently they reached the edge of the woods. The wagon road they had followed the night before ran all the way through the stretch and a break in the trees a short distance away showed where it came out on that side.

"We must go carefully now," warned Hugh. "How far in is the old house?"

"Oh, about a quarter of a mile," said Bob. "I don't believe any one is apt to be out here in the daytime." He felt for his back pocket, however, and the knowledge that he had a revolver with him was most reassuring.

They stole along through the woods, stepping softly and keeping a sharp lookout in all directions. All was silent, however, and seemingly they were alone. Before long they were able to glimpse the old deserted house through the trees. They stopped and gazed at it intently.

It was two stories high and of wood. Years had evidently passed since any one had lived there and the house was in need of repairing. Some of the shutters were missing, others sagged or were hanging limply from the frames, the glass in most of the windows was broken, and the wind and weather had stripped practically all the paint from the sides of the abandoned dwelling. The cellar door was missing and all in all the place presented a forlorn and desolate appearance. Hugh and Bob both recalled tales of ghosts connected with the old house, and somehow now that they were there they wished they had stayed at home.

"Perhaps we ought to report this business to the police after all," whispered Hugh.

"Yes," said Bob. "Still I'd hate to go home and tell father that we didn't even go inside the place."

"That's true," Hugh agreed. "What shall we do?"

"Let's walk around it and see if we can see anything suspicious."

"All right. We'd better keep in the shelter of the woods though."

"Oh, yes, of course."

Remaining almost a hundred feet distant from the little clearing, in the center of which stood the house, the boys began to walk. Save for an occasional nervous glance about them they never took their eyes off the deserted dwelling. When they came to the wagon-road they darted across quickly, fearful lest they should be discovered. Their progress was slow and an hour had elapsed when they returned to their starting point.

"I don't believe any one is there," whispered Bob.

"It doesn't look so. Shall we go in?"

"I suppose so," said Bob, though it was plain to be seen that neither boy much relished the task. However they dared not go home and report failure to Mr. Cook, so presently they ventured forth from the woods and started across the clearing. The cellar door was open and toward this they made their way.

A gentle breeze rattled one of the shutters, causing the boys to start nervously. Bob kept his hand on his hip pocket and they walked closely together. Presently they came to the cellar steps and peered in cautiously. Their faces were pale, as gingerly they walked down the stone steps and entered the gloomy cellar.

"Flash your light," whispered Bob.

Hugh did so, and a huge gray rat scuttled across the floor, startling the boys so that they almost cried out. Little by little their courage returned, however, and they advanced a few steps. They listened intently, but no sound came to their ears. Hugh's flashlight revealed the stairs leading to the first floor and stepping noiselessly the boys approached.

Slowly and very cautiously they ascended and presently came to the top of the stairs. Bob was in the lead, his pistol gripped tightly in one hand. With his free hand he pushed the door open gently and looked within. The kitchen was deserted, a broken-down stove in one corner, a water heater covered with dirt and rust, a sagging sink, and two battered chairs and a table completing the furnishings. A soft breeze entered through a broken window and gently stirred the strip of wall paper hanging limply from the ceiling.

Bob beckoned to Hugh and they emerged into the room. They listened intently. Not a sound was to be heard. Reassured they passed out of the kitchen through a narrow back hall, and into the parlor. The same aspect of neglect and decay was everywhere evident, but nothing suspicious was to be seen.

"Shall we go upstairs?" whispered Bob.

"We might as well. I don't believe there's any one here anyway."

The stairs leading to the second floor creaked and groaned under the weight of the boys, but as they were now convinced that the house was uninhabited they were not worried. Coming to the second story they proceeded to the room located in the front of the house.

"This must be the place," whispered Bob excitedly.

A table stood in the center of the room; around it were grouped five seats, chairs and old boxes, as if five men had had a meeting or conference there.

"This is where they had their meeting last night," said Hugh. "Here are places for five men, and we saw that many come out."

"Yes, sir," echoed Bob. "This looks like headquarters."

"Suppose we could expose them," exclaimed Hugh. "Wouldn't it be great?"

"If we only could," said Bob eagerly. "Let's look around."

Pen and ink, together with a pad of writing paper were lying on the table. Besides the table and seats, however, there was no furniture in the room, and there seemed small promise of anything of interest to the two searchers. They lifted every box and searched under it, but all in vain. Finally Bob looked behind the door. With an exclamation of delight he stooped and picked up a piece of paper lying upon the floor.

"What is it, Bob?" inquired Hugh eagerly.

"I don't know. I can't see very well."

"Bring it over here by the window. It's awfully dark and gloomy in this room."

Bob followed this suggestion, and presently was reading what was written on the paper. Hugh looked on over his shoulder.

"'List of places to be attacked.'" Bob read. "'Railroad bridge, Court House, Armory, National Cartridge Company, High Ridge Steel Company. More to be added later.'"

"This looks like the real thing," exclaimed Bob excitedly. "I wonder if they plan to take these in order. At any rate we fooled them once on the railroad bridge."

"Yes," said Hugh, "and we want to fool them on the others if we can."

"They've got father's factory listed," exclaimed Bob. "I was afraid they would; the Germans don't like him. He's too good an American."

"Some one must have dropped that paper by mistake," said Hugh. "They never would have left anything like that lying around."

"Suppose they discover they've left it and come back after it."

Both boys looked nervously out of the window, but all they saw was the little clearing and the quiet trees, swaying gently under the light breeze.

"Isn't it signed?" asked Hugh.

"No."

"Look on the back; there may be something there."

Bob turned over the sheet of paper. "No writing," he said. "There's a picture here though."

"What is it?"

"I can't see very well. It looks like some sort of a bug."

"It looks like an alligator," said Hugh, taking the paper from Bob and examining it closely.

"Let me see," exclaimed Bob. "That's what it is," he announced a moment later. "What do you suppose is the idea of that?"

"I'm sure I don't know. Probably some man was just trying to amuse himself by drawing pictures, and happened to draw an alligator."

"Maybe it's a picture of Percy," laughed Bob.

"Say," exclaimed Hugh suddenly, "it's strange, though.

Heinie's alligator was probably stolen by the man that returned the car, and whoever returned the car was probably out here at this meeting. What's the connection?"

"I don't believe there is any," said Bob. "You're too suspicious, Hugh."

"Won't you admit that it's queer?"

"Of course I will, but I think it also proves that Heinie couldn't have been the one who returned our car last night. That is, if you think the man who stole the alligator was the one who brought back the car. Heinrich wouldn't cry about the loss of his pet if he was the one who took it, would he?"

"It's too deep for one to understand," sighed Hugh with a shake of his head. "At any rate one thing is sure and that is that some plots are being hatched around here and -"

Before he could finish there was a loud crash behind them, the only door leading out of the room was slammed shut, and a key turned in the lock.

CHAPTER XII

TRAPPED

Bob and Hugh stared at each other in astonishment. They had been tricked and were now prisoners. A moment later they recovered somewhat from their surprise and with one accord sprang for the door.

Bob seized the knob and shook it violently. To no purpose, however.

"Get a chair, Hugh," he cried. "We'll smash the door in."

"How do we know what's waiting for us in the hall?"

"I don't care. We've got to get out of here."

There was a deafening report of a gun fired in the narrow hall. The panel of the door close to Bob's head was splintered, and a bullet shot across the room, shivering the one remaining pane of glass left in the window.

"Duck!" shouted Hugh. "Get away from that door!"

Bob needed no second urging. He sprang aside and cowered against the side of the wall. The two boys looked at each other, pale-lipped and breathing hard.

"Whew," exclaimed Hugh. "That was a close call."

Bob whipped his pistol out of his pocket, and began to crawl back toward the door.

"What are you going to do?" demanded Hugh in alarm.

"I'm going to send a bullet through there myself," said Bob. "We might just as well let them know we're alive too."

"Don't you do it. You'll only waste your bullets and it may help us later if they don't know we are armed."

Bob hesitated. "I guess you're right," he said a moment later, and presently resumed his place against the wall.

"What'll we do?" said Hugh.

"I don't know. Did you hear anybody?"

"Not a soul. All I heard was the door bang and then the pistol shot."

"I guess we're in for it," said Bob nervously.

"We must get out of here."

"I think so too, but how?"

"We can smash the door."

"Yes, and the minute we stick our heads out of the door we'll get a bullet through us. I don't see that we stand a chance."

"But we can't stay here," protested Hugh. "If we do they'll certainly fix us one way or another."

"If I don't come home to lunch father will get worried and bring help to us; he knows where we are."

"These people won't wait that long. If they are spies and plotters they'll be desperate and they won't waste much time dealing with us."

"I wonder how far it is to the ground."

"We'd break a leg trying to jump," said Hugh.

"I'll look anyway," and Bob carefully raised himself to his feet and advanced toward the window. He peered out and then suddenly uttered an exclamation.

"Hugh," he cried in a low voice. "The gray roadster is out there. A man just got in and is driving off."

With one bound Hugh was by his friend's side. "Could you see who it was?" he demanded eagerly. The roadster had disappeared down the wagon road.

"I couldn't see," said Bob. "His back was toward me all the time."

"How do you suppose that car got in here without our hearing it?"

"I don't know. Of course they had the cutout closed."

"Do you think that man has gone for help?"

"I wouldn't be surprised."

"Then now is our chance to get out of here."

"Perhaps he left a guard."

"I can't help it. At any rate we'll never have a better opportunity than this."

"Shall we smash the door in with a chair?" asked Bob.

"I don't see what else we can do."

"It's a chance."

"Of course it is, but it's no bigger chance than it is to stay here."

"All right then," said Bob. "Let's each get a chair."

They possessed themselves of chairs and then took their places one on each side of the door. They held the chairs by the backs and prepared to swing them against the panels.

"One, two, three," counted Bob, and smote the door with all the strength he could muster. A second later Hugh followed suit. The door was made of heavy oak, however, and stood fast. Bob and Hugh shrank back against the wall and waited for any result of their efforts. Silence pervaded the house.

"I guess that man was the only one here," said Hugh.

"It seems so; let's try it again."

Once more the chairs crashed against the door, but without effect. Again and again the two boys exerted themselves to the utmost, but the sole result of their efforts was to break the chairs. Finally, well-nigh exhausted, they stopped.

"It's no use, Bob," panted Hugh. "The door is stronger than the chairs."

"We've got to get out of here though."

"The only way I can see is the window."

"But we can't jump that far; we'd only break a leg or something. There isn't even a roof to help us."

"Can't we make a rope out of our clothes and slide down?"

"I say to try the door again," exclaimed Bob.

"But we can't smash it with these chairs," Hugh protested.

"I know it; let's try the table."

"How are you going to do that?"

"I'll show you," said Bob. "Take hold of this end with me."

They grasped the table and dragged it to a spot directly in front of the door and eight or ten feet distant from it. "Now," exclaimed Bob. "When I say, 'three,' we'll push it with all our might against the door."

"It'll never work," said Hugh, with a shake of his head.

"Try it," cried Bob. "We've got to do something."

They took firm hold of the table and set themselves. "Now," said Bob. "One, two, three." They pushed with all their strength and a moment later the table crashed into the door. The door creaked and groaned but did not give way.

"It won't work," said Hugh with great conviction.

"Yes, it will too," exclaimed Bob. "Stick to it."

They dragged the table back and once again drove it hurtling against the door. This time their efforts met with some success for the corner of the table drove straight through one of the panels.

"See that?" cried Bob excitedly. "I believe that if I put my hand through that opening I can reach the key and unlock the door."

"You don't suppose for a second that that man left the key in the door, do you?"

"I don't suppose he did," admitted Bob, somewhat crestfallen. "Still there's no harm in trying anyway."

"There may be somebody on guard in the hall."

"We'll have to risk that." Bob thrust his arm through the opening made in the door panel, but soon withdrew it. "The key is not there," he said.

"Of course not," exclaimed Hugh. "Get out of the way

and let me get a few whacks at that panel with the chair." He attacked the door furiously and in a few moments had knocked out the panel completely.

"I guess we can squeeze through there now," he said.

"Let me go first," exclaimed Bob. "I've got a gun."

He squirmed through the opening in the door and seeing no sign of any one outside called to Hugh to follow him. A moment later they stood side by side in the dark and narrow hallway.

"We'd better get out of here as fast as we can," whispered Bob.

"The sooner it is, the better I'm pleased," returned Hugh grimly.

They stole along the hall, every sense alert. Presently they came to the head of the stairs and discovering nothing to alarm them, started down. The stairs still creaked and groaned, but the boys' confidence was rapidly returning as they neared outdoors and safety, and they hurried along.

A side door stood open and toward this they made their way. Bob had returned his revolver to his pocket for he really thought he should not need it any more. He stepped out of the doorway and started down the steps. As he did so a man sprang at him and with a blackjack dealt him a stunning blow over the head. Bob reeled uncertainly for an instant, and then sank unconscious to the floor; there he lay in a limp heap.

Before the man could deal with Bob's companion,

Hugh had grappled with him, and a moment later they were rolling over and over on the ground fighting like wild cats.

CHAPTER XIII

MISTAKEN IDENTITY

Hugh had seized the man by his right wrist and as they went down the blackjack was sent spinning. It was man to man, bare hands for weapons.

Hugh's assailant was not large, but he was extremely agile. He squirmed and wriggled, kicked and butted, in fact he used every weapon at his command. Hugh probably outweighed his enemy, and in addition was a splendid wrestler, but he was young and his antagonist's strength was more developed.

Each fighter struggled desperately to get an arm free. Once Hugh succeeded, but it was his left arm, and when he seized his opponent's throat his hold was soon shaken loose. They fought fiercely, both breathing hard, their faces were red and blotched, and their eyes were staring. Over and over they rolled, the stones and twigs on the ground tearing and lacerating their hands and faces.

Hugh got hold of his opponent's right arm. He bent it back with every bit of strength he possessed, until the man cried out in pain. Hugh knew, however, that he would receive no mercy if he was overcome and he pressed home his advantage. Suddenly, with a convulsive twist of his body, the man shook loose Hugh's hold, and dealt him a heavy blow in the chest. Hugh felt his wind badly shaken and he seized his opponent around the waist with both arms, squeezing with all the strength in his body. His one idea was to keep as close to his enemy as he could, so that the man would have no opportunity to strike him again.

Gradually Hugh felt his strength slipping. He knew he could not hold out much longer, and even as he struggled he wondered how soon it would be before the other Germans returned and made an end of him. Then when he least expected it, help came to him.

Bob had opened his eyes after a moment. He had seen millions of stars, and as he came to his senses again his head felt sore and battered. He did not recall for a moment just what had befallen him. Suddenly, however, he heard the sounds of a violent struggle being waged near at hand, and sitting up he spied Hugh and his assailant locked in each other's grasp, and still fighting. Bob sprang to his feet and approached them.

He remembered everything now. His throbbing head recalled to him the blow he had received and he could feel a large lump on the back of it. He wondered what would have happened to him if he had not worn a hat. A moment later, however, he had dismissed from his mind all thought of himself and was engaged in assisting his friend.

He grasped Hugh's assailant by his throat and knelt on his shoulders with both knees. Gradually the man's strength waned; Hugh could feel it slipping. A moment later he lay gasping on the ground too weak to offer any resistance to the two boys. Hugh held his arms, while Bob released his hold on the man's throat and sat on his legs. The prisoner, his breath rattling in his chest, lay with eyes half-closed, completely done up.

Suddenly Hugh spied something that made him start violently. The man's coat lay wide open and pinned on his vest was a badge. More than that, it was a police badge, one of the badges of the police of High Ridge.

"Bob," gasped Hugh in alarm, "this man's a detective."

"What!" cried Bob. "You're crazy."

"I am not. Look here."

He released his hold on his erstwhile opponent and stood up. Bob followed suit. In amazement they looked at the man on the ground at their feet.

"That's a High Ridge police badge all right," said Bob. "No doubt of it."

"Are you a detective?" Hugh asked their victim.

The man looked at them through narrowed eyelids. "Yes," he said weakly, and started to reach towards his hip pocket.

"Here, here!" cried Hugh. "None of that! This whole thing is a mistake."

"Let me help you up," urged Bob, offering his hand to the beaten man. Hugh also assisted him and they raised him to his feet.

"I guess we were after the same people you were,"

exclaimed Bob, taking it for granted that the detective had trailed the Germans to the deserted house as he and Hugh had done. "They had us locked up in there and we had just broken down the door and were coming out. We didn't know you were a detective."

"You didn't give us a chance to find out," laughed Hugh, greatly relieved at the unexpected turn of events. He also felt safer to have an officer of the law with them.

The detective rubbed his neck, and looked at the two boys narrowly.

"Germans in this house?" he said at length.

"They had a meeting here last night," said Bob.

"How do you know?"

"We followed them out here. Look at this too," and he handed over the list of buildings to be destroyed that they had found in the old house.

The detective snatched the paper out of his hand and scanned it eagerly.

"Where did you get this?" he demanded.

"We found it upstairs," said Bob.

"Humph," ejaculated the detective and thrust it into his pocket.

"Weren't you trailing these Germans too?" inquired Bob.

"How do you know they were Germans?"

"Who else would want to blow up bridges and ammunition factories?"

"Did they intend to do that?"

"That's what that list says," exclaimed Hugh, nettled by the questions the man asked as well as by his odd behavior.

"Well," said the detective, "you take my advice. This is no place for a couple of boys like you to be hanging around. You might get hurt the first thing you know." He glanced about him nervously as though he expected some one else to arrive upon the scene at any moment.

"A man locked us in that room just before you arrived," said Bob. "Then he dashed off in a big gray roadster."

"Well, you'd better get out of here yourselves," said the detective shortly.

"They may come back at any minute and perhaps you'll need help," protested Bob.

"I'll take care of that part of it," exclaimed the detective. "You get out."

Convinced that there was nothing else for them to do, Bob and Hugh started off through the woods, leaving the detective in undisputed possession of the premises. They were greatly puzzled by their recent experience.

"What do you think of that detective?" demanded Bob,

when they had reached a point out of sight of the house.

"I think he was an old grouch," exclaimed Hugh. "I don't see why he had to be so disagreeable to us; all we wanted to do was to help him."

"Yes, when those Germans come back he's apt to be handled roughly."

"He was jealous of us, I believe," said Bob.

"Why so?"

"Well, we had gone ahead on our own account, and from the way he acted I guess we knew more about what was going on than he did."

"Perhaps that's it," said Hugh. "Maybe he was afraid we might take some glory away from him."

"How silly!" exclaimed Bob. "What do we want with glory?"

"We'd better tell your father what happened this morning."

"Of course. He'll think I'm a pretty poor fighter though; a black eye one day and a big lump on my head the next."

"How does your head feel anyway?" inquired Hugh.

"Oh, pretty well. It still throbs though."

"I should think it might, and you can consider yourself

pretty lucky that you didn't get your skull cracked open."

"He was a queer looking man, wasn't he?"

"Yes, and his actions were even queerer."

"I guess he was jealous," said Bob. "Oh, well, I don't suppose it makes any difference who corners those Germans, so long as somebody does it."

"Personally, I'm sort of glad to get away from that house," said Hugh. "I believe that if we had stayed much longer we never would have left."

"How about the detective?"

"If he wants to stay that's his lookout, not ours."

"That's right, and I suppose he'll go for help anyway."

"Perhaps they'll just watch the house for a day or two," said Hugh. "It may be though that now that those Germans know they are watched they may meet in some other place."

"True enough. I wish we could find the place."

Presently they came to the spot where they had left their bicycles. They were still there, and a moment later the boys were wheeling them back across the field again. Once more in the road, they mounted and soon were riding towards home. Their minds were busy with plots and Germans and the recent experiences they had undergone. They felt sure that they were on the trail of a desperate gang, and that quick action perhaps was necessary to prevent untold damage, and possible loss of life.

They were confused, however. Everywhere they turned they seemed to run into some new angle of the affair, or some other person who might bear watching. Hugh was still of the opinion that Heinrich and Lena should be looked after pretty carefully, though Bob laughed at him. He knew his family felt that their servants could be relied upon absolutely. Bob wondered about his father's plant; was it properly guarded? Perhaps his father might consent to let him go down there and help watch over it at night.

Talking but little they spun along the road. Each boy was occupied with his own thoughts, and consequently did not notice an automobile rapidly approaching down the road.

"Here comes a car," exclaimed Bob suddenly. They swung over to the right side of the road to let it pass, and a moment later it roared past them in a cloud of dust.

"Bob," cried Hugh excitedly. "The gray roadster."

"I know it. Did you see who was in it?"

"I didn't notice."

"Mr. Wernberg."

"What!"

"It certainly was."

"I guess your father was right about him then. He said he was a dangerous man, and I guess he is, if he's mixed up with that gang out there."

"Well, Frank wouldn't talk the way he does unless he'd heard it at home."

"Probably not. Do you suppose they recognized us?"

"Suppose they did?" said Bob, carelessly. "We have a right to the road, haven't we?"

"Certainly, but the man who locked us in the room! He must have been in the car and would surely recognize us as the ones who were in the house."

"That's true," exclaimed Bob. "Do you think they'll turn around and come after us?"

Hugh glanced back over his shoulder. "The car has stopped," he exclaimed. "Come on, Bob, we'd better ride for all there is in us."

The two boys leaned forward on their pedals, bent low over the handlebars, and rode as hard as they could. They were not far from the town now and they knew that the occupants of the gray roadster would not dare molest them, when once they had gained the populated districts. Not once did they look back until they were safely within the city limits.

"I didn't think they'd follow us," puffed Hugh. "Still it's just as well to take no chances."

"I wasn't so much afraid of them chasing us," said Bob. "What worries me is that probably they know who we are now, and consequently we won't be safe no matter where we are."

"I guess we'll have to report to the police."

"If we do I hope they treat us better than that detective did."

"I hope so, too," laughed Hugh. "At any rate we'll ask your father."

"You are coming to our house for luncheon, you know."

"Yes."

"We can talk it over with father then."

They arrived at the Cook residence without further adventure or mishap. They left their bicycles in the garage, and then started for the house. Half-way across the lawn they met Mr. Cook.

"Well, boys," he said, plainly relieved at seeing them safely back, "what luck?"

"Feel my head," said Bob, removing his cap.

Mr. Cook did so. "Whew!" he exclaimed. "Where did you get that?"

Bob related the story of their experiences that morning. Mr. Cook offered no comment until he had finished. "This looks serious," he said at length. "It's too bad you got such a bump from a detective, a man on your own side."

"What do you think of our seeing Mr. Wernberg?" asked Hugh.

Mr. Cook's face clouded and he shook his head. "I was afraid of him," he said.

"What shall we do about it?" Bob inquired.

"I think we'd better report it to the police, and do it soon, too." He looked at his watch. "We've got time before luncheon," he exclaimed. "Was Heinrich in the garage?"

"No, sir."

"How about the car?"

"That's there all right."

"Well, come along then," exclaimed Mr. Cook. "We'll get it and go straight down to police headquarters now."

"Don't you think our friend the detective will make a report?" asked Hugh.

"Possibly. Still, as Bob says, those men are sometimes very jealous and he might not tell the whole story, particularly about what you did."

A few moments later all three were on their way to the police station. Bob's old friend, Sergeant Riley, was still behind the desk and gave them a jovial greeting.

"Yez haven't got no Germans for me, have yez?" he demanded.

"No," said Mr. Cook, "we haven't, but we can tell you where to get some."

"Sounds interesting," said the sergeant laying aside his pen and carefully blotting the sheet of paper on which he had been writing. "Tell me about it."

"Go ahead, Bob," his father urged. "Tell your story, and first of all let Sergeant Riley feel the bump on your head. That'll convince him."

"It would indade," exclaimed the sergeant, after examining the swelling on Bob's head. "Not that I'd ever doubt anything a son of yours told me, Misther Cook."

Bob related the events of that day to Sergeant Riley. The police officer listened attentively and interestedly until Bob came to the part about the detective. As he began to tell of that the sergeant started perceptibly.

"A detective, yez said?" he demanded.

"Yes," said Bob, "he had a badge on."

"Can yez describe him?"

"Well," said Bob, "he was a man about five feet seven inches tall; he had dark hair and a close-cut black mustache. I should think he would weigh possibly about a hundred and fifty pounds; maybe not quite so much. He had on a soft brown hat and a dark suit of clothes. I can't remember anything more about him."

"That's a plenty," exclaimed the sergeant. He had been jotting down the description of the detective as

Bob spoke.

"He was a grouchy fellow all right," exclaimed Hugh. "He chased us away from there as though he was jealous of us and didn't want us around."

"I daresay he didn't want yez," said Riley.

"What's his name?" asked Bob.

"I don't know," replied the sergeant.

"Come on, Riley," laughed Mr. Cook, "you can't tell me that. Why I thought you knew every one in High Ridge to say nothing of your own force. You don't mean to tell me you don't know a detective that wears the same badge you do?"

"Yes, sir, I do," said Riley soberly. "And I'll tell yez why. That man these boys met this morning is no detective at all."

CHAPTER XIV

AN EXPEDITION

Mr. Cook and the two boys were so completely taken aback by the sergeant's statement that for a moment all they could do was stare at one another in amazement. Bob was the first to regain his voice.

"What do you mean, Sergeant?" he demanded.

"Just what I say."

"That man was not a detective?" stammered Bob. "He is not a member of the High Ridge force?"

"There is no man answering to that description here."

"Then he was a fake."

"Exactly."

"Well," exclaimed Hugh, Bob, and Mr. Cook in one breath. They could say no more.

"He was a fake," repeated Sergeant Riley emphatically. "There is no doubt of it."

The boys were too surprised for words. What kind of a

Paul G. Tomlinson

business was this they were becoming involved in anyway? The further they went the more confused they became. If you could not trust a man with a regulation police badge, whom could you trust?

"It seems incredible," said Mr. Cook.

"We are at war with Germany, aren't we?" asked Sergeant Riley calmly.

"We are," Mr. Cook agreed.

"Well, then," said the sergeant, "that explains it. They want to do us all the harm they can and as they can't bring soldiers over here, thanks to the English fleet, they've got to strike at us with plots and bombs and such things. They will stop at nothing."

"Are there many to guard against in High Ridge?" asked Mr. Cook. "You know I am interested because my factory is making ammunition for the Government."

"There are several," the sergeant admitted.

"Can you tell me who they are?"

"I cannot. 'Twould be against my orders. Yez might feel better to know that we are watching them pretty carefully though."

"I hope so," said Mr. Cook fervently.

"Have yez had lunch?" asked the sergeant suddenly.

"No," replied Mr. Cook. "Not yet."

"Well, suppose yez go home and get it. I may telephone yez a little later to go out to that house with some of our men."

"Good," cried Mr. Cook. "We'll hurry and you may be sure we'll be ready any time you call on us."

They left the police station and were soon on their way home. Arriving at the house, Hugh and Mr. Cook got out, and Bob drove the car down to the garage. There he found Heinrich seated on a box in one corner intently studying a sheet of paper he held in his hand.

"What you got, Heinie?" asked Bob cheerily. "A love letter!"

Heinrich looked up at Bob, a curious expression in his pale blue eyes. He made no comment, however, and presently returned to the perusal of the paper he held.

"What is it?" demanded Bob, impressed by the chauffeur's manner. An air of gloom seemed to pervade the garage, even the dog, the cat, and the parrot appeared to be affected by it. The dog stood listlessly by his master's side, the cat walked idly up and down, and the bird failed to greet Bob with his usual cheery "How do"; he sat limply on his perch, his feathers ruffled, and muttered to himself.

Heinrich handed the paper to Bob. It was a sheet evidently torn from a pad and in a large scrawling hand was written the following: "We warned your boss to keep his car at home; now tell him to keep his son there, too." No name was signed and Bob turned the paper over and looked at the opposite side. A picture of an alligator was drawn there. Bob recognized the sheet as similar to the one that he and Hugh had found in the deserted house and the detective had taken from them; apparently it had been torn from the same pad.

"Where did you get this, Heinie?" he demanded.

"I go up to the house to see Lena," said Heinrich. "That is maybe a half-hour ago. I only stay there a few minutes and when I come back here is this."

"Lying on the floor?"

"Yes."

"Have you no idea who sent it?"

"How should I?" exclaimed Heinrich.

"Somebody must have slipped in here while you were absent and left it," said Bob. "There are queer things happening around here these days, Heinie."

"There is," the chauffeur admitted solemnly.

"Do you mind if I keep this paper?"

"No."

Bob started out.

"You better do as that says, too," exclaimed Heinrich earnestly. "You would not want anything to happen to you."

"I'm not afraid," said Bob soberly. "You know, Heinie," he continued, "some people are trying to blow up things around here. Some of your countrymen, and we can't let them do anything like that, you know."

Heinrich seemed much perturbed at this. "So?" he exclaimed his eyes wide.

"Yes," said Bob, "and it's men like you who ought to stop them. You men who were Germans but are now Americans, could do yourselves a good turn if you did. Some people of German blood are under suspicion nowadays and if you showed that you were loyal to the United States it would be a good thing for you. Not that I mean to say we are suspicious of *you*," Bob hastened to add.

This speech of Bob's seemed to offer a new line of thought to Heinrich who merely stared at Bob and said nothing.

"Heinrich is so loyal himself that it never occurred to him that any one would be suspicious," thought Bob as he hurried off toward the house, the strange paper clutched tightly in one hand.

He arrived to find every one at the dining-table, and consequently he said nothing about the warning, for he did not wish to alarm his mother. She had just heard from Harold; his company had been ordered away from High Ridge that morning for an unknown destination. She was worried enough over that without having another son on her mind. Fortunately the lump on Bob's head was covered by his hair so that it was not noticeable enough to draw attention to it. His black eye already had been explained.

Luncheon was hardly over when the telephone

Paul G. Tomlinson

summoned Mr. Cook. Sergeant Riley was on the wire inquiring if Mr. Cook and Bob and Hugh could not meet him at headquarters immediately. A few moments later they were in the car and on their way down the street. Bob was at the wheel.

Another car was drawn up alongside the curb in front of the police station and in it were four plain-clothes men. Sergeant Riley was there to explain that they planned to go out to the deserted house and search it thoroughly, by force if necessary. He wished the two boys to go along as guides, and he thought probably Mr. Cook would want to accompany them.

A short time later they started, Bob leading the way. As they passed Elm Street he glanced curiously at the white stucco house, number twelve eighty two, and wondered what had happened to the German who had attempted to destroy the railroad bridge. Probably he now rested in jail, awaiting trial. Then again it occurred to Bob that possibly he had been shot; the country was at war and offenders of that kind were not dealt lightly with at such a time.

They left the city behind and rolled along over the country road. The three occupants of the car were silent for they did not know what might await them at their destination. A squad of soldiers out on a hike passed them. They were hot, dirty and dusty, but their rifles glinted wickedly in the light of the afternoon sun.

"They look like business," remarked Mr. Cook.

"They certainly do," exclaimed Bob. "I wish I was one of them."

"If the war lasts long enough maybe you will be."

"The United States can certainly raise a big army."

"Indeed it can," his father agreed. "Germany thought they'd have nothing to fear from us, but they'll be sadly fooled. Just think of the money and food and equipment of all kinds we can furnish our allies; those things are just as important as men, and we can send millions of those, too, if they need them."

Presently they came to the spot where Bob and Hugh had dismounted from their bicycles that morning. Bob stopped the car and the plain-clothes detectives followed suit. Sergeant Riley took charge.

"You lead the way," he said to Bob. "We'll follow wherever you go."

A moment later they were off across the field and soon came to the woods which sheltered the deserted house. In Indian file they commenced to pick their path among the trees and underbrush. Complete silence was maintained and the party advanced, ready for any emergency. Of course the detectives were armed. Mr. Cook carried his pistol, so Bob and Hugh were the only ones not provided with some means of defense.

In the course of perhaps fifteen minutes Bob, from his position in the lead, caught a glimpse of the old house through the trees. So far as he could see there was no sign of life around it anywhere. He held up his hand and the little party came to a halt. A whispered consultation was held and it was decided to spread out somewhat and move forward in open order.

The plan was to advance until they reached the border of the trees, and then at a given signal rush out into the opening and surround the house. Stealthily the band stole forward. The spring air was soft and balmy, the buds on the trees were commencing to swell; everywhere nature gave signs of a reawakening, but these things passed unnoticed. The members of the little party were occupied with the business in hand, and had no time or interest for anything else.

Soon they reached their appointed positions. From the spot where he crouched Bob could see the others lurking within the shelter of the trees. He could see Sergeant Riley raising a police whistle to his lips to sound the signal that had been agreed upon. Bob set himself. He had been advised that inasmuch as he was unarmed he should remain behind, but he had no such intention. Neither had Hugh.

Suddenly Sergeant Riley sounded a shrill blast with his whistle. Every man rushed forward. Only for a few steps, however. A burst of flame, and a puff of smoke shot from the cellar window of the old house, and the air was rent by a terrific explosion.

CHAPTER XV

FIRE

Staggered, the men all stopped short in their tracks. An instant later there was a second explosion. There was a ripping, splitting sound, and the whole side of the building fell out. The air was filled with bits of wood and plaster.

"Keep away from that house!" shouted Sergeant Riley as one of his men darted forward. "Do yez want to get killed?"

A minute later flames appeared, and the red and yellow tongues of fire began to play around the window frames. Black smoke curled from every opening. It was plainly to be seen that the house was doomed.

"Look!" cried Hugh suddenly. "There goes a man!"

Without waiting to see what the others were going to do he dashed off in pursuit of a figure which could be seen scuttling away through the trees. Two of the detectives joined in the race and one of them fired two shots from his pistol at the fugitive. In reply the man suddenly wheeled and shot once at his pursuers. Bob heard the bullet whine past close to his head. He also had caught a fleeting glimpse of the man, and one look was enough to convince him that it was the fake detective with whom he and Hugh had struggled that morning.

A moment later the man was out of sight, Hugh and the two detectives still after him, shouting and calling to him to halt. Meanwhile the fire in the house roared and blazed.

"She's a goner," said Sergeant Riley. He stood beside Mr. Cook and Bob as they watched the burning building.

"I guess she is," remarked Mr. Cook. "There's nothing we can do."

"Nothing," agreed the sergeant.

"It's not much loss anyway," said Mr. Cook.

"No loss at all," exclaimed Bob. "It's a gain if any-thing, for it makes one less place for spies and plotters to meet in."

"But any evidence that might have been in there is destroyed," said Riley.

"I never thought of that," said Bob. "That's probably why they burned it."

"Was that your detective running off through the woods?" asked the sergeant.

"It certainly was," said Bob. "I guess he was one of the gang after all. I suppose they left him behind to watch us."

"Then why did he let you get away?" his father replied.

"Probably he thought it would create less suspicion," said Sergeant Riley. "He got the paper away from the boys and as long as he thought he could bluff them into thinking he was a detective he thought that was sufficient. On the other hand if he had held them prisoners or anything like that there would have been a search for them and trouble started at once."

"I guess that's right," said Mr. Cook soberly. "However, I hope they catch him this time."

Suddenly a piercing scream startled them. They glanced up to see a white face at one of the windows of the house. All around, the fire roared and the smoke curled up in great clouds. Before they could see who the man was he had fallen back into the room and disappeared from view.

"I'll get him," exclaimed one of the detectives, and without further ado, he sprinted for the burning house. Paying no heed to the warning cries of his comrades he dashed up to the back door and entered, and was soon lost to sight.

"That feller Donovan is a dare-devil," exclaimed Sergeant Riley. "He'll stop at nothing. Why should he risk his life for a man that's as good as dead now?"

"He'll never come out alive," cried Mr. Cook.

"And all for a man who is plotting against the country," echoed Riley. "Here you!" he shouted to the other plain-clothes man. "Keep out of there. The High Ridge police force can't afford to lose more than one man a day." The fourth detective showed signs of wishing to follow his comrade.

"If he does rescue that man it'll only be to put him in jail," said Bob.

"Or shoot him more likely," cried Riley angrily.

Breathless they waited for any sign of Donovan. The fire burned more fiercely every moment, and it seemed incredible that any man could enter that seething furnace and return alive. The air was filled with sparks and blazing embers; the smoke mounted heavenward in a thick column which must have been visible for miles.

Minutes that seemed like hours passed. Hugh and the two detectives returned from their chase. They had not captured their man.

"We followed him as far as the road," one of them reported. "He had a motor cycle there and got away from us."

"We'll get him later, never fear," said Sergeant Riley, grimly. "Meanwhile that crazy man, Donovan, is in the house here trying to rescue some one of them German plotters that showed his face at the window."

The recipients of this piece of news gasped. "He'll never come out," exclaimed one of the men. "Still, he never did seem to care much for his life."

White faced and tense they watched the conflagration. Certainly not one of the men ever expected to see Donovan again. Yet what could they do? As Sergeant

Riley had said, it was folly for any one else to follow him in, and so they were powerless. All they could do was watch and hope.

Suddenly a figure appeared at the door. It seemed to issue straight from the hottest part of the fire. On its shoulder was the limp figure of a man.

"There he is!" cried six voices together, and together the six watchers made for the house.

Donovan, for it was he, stood on the charred steps. Sparks and blazing firebrands fell all around him and he tottered uncertainly. Willing helpers rushed to his assistance, but before they could reach him he swayed and fell. He rolled down the step dropping his burden, and side by side the two men lay on the ground. Close by, the wall threatened to fall on them at any moment.

It did not take long to seize both men, and carry them away from danger and a moment later they were stretched out side by side on the grass, a safe distance from the burning building.

The man whom Donovan had rescued, had a face so blackened by smoke and soot that he was unrecognizable. His clothes were scorched and his whole body seared with terrible burns. He was unconscious.

"Is he still alive?" whispered Bob in a low voice.

Sergeant Riley put his hand over the wounded man's heart. "I think so," he said. "Get some water somebody. And look after Donovan."

"There's a spring back there in the woods," exclaimed Hugh. "I have nothing to carry water in though."

"Take all the handkerchiefs you can get," ordered the sergeant. "Fill the hats; you'll lose most of it on the way back, but you'll get some."

Hugh hastened to obey; with him went Bob and two of the detectives. The spring was not far distant, and they soon were sousing the handkerchiefs in the clear, cold water. The hats, too, were filled and those made of felt held the water fairly well. A few moments later they were hurrying back toward the spot where the injured man was lying.

It had been found necessary to remove the patients farther away from the burning building, for the heat grew more intense every moment. Donovan had so far recovered as to be sitting up. He suffered acutely from numerous burns, but otherwise seemed to be all right. The man whom he had rescued, however, still lay unconscious on the ground.

Sergeant Riley now took charge of the operations. He bathed Donovan's face with one of the handkerchiefs and gave him another to suck. Mr. Cook under Riley's instructions poured water from one of the hats upon the other sufferer's face, and then gently sopped it with a handkerchief. As a result of this treatment the soot and grime disappeared and presently it was possible to distinguish his features.

Suddenly Mr. Cook started back in surprise. "Come here, Bob," he cried. "See who this is."

One glance was enough for Bob. He recognized the

man over whom his father was working as Mr. Wernberg.

Paul G. Tomlinson

CHAPTER XVI

MORE COMPLICATIONS

"Who is he?" inquired Sergeant Riley, noting his companion's astonishment.

"His name is Wernberg," said Mr. Cook.

"I've heard of him," said Riley grimly.

"Have you been looking for him?"

"I know his name," exclaimed the sergeant evasively.

"Well," said Mr. Cook, "he's about done for, I'm afraid. I suppose we ought to get him to a doctor as fast as we can though."

"Yes," agreed Riley.

"I'll get our car," exclaimed Bob.

"Can you bring it in here?" asked his father.

"Yes. I'll have it here in ten minutes," and Bob set off at top speed through the woods toward the spot where the automobile had been left.

Mr. Wernberg was still unconscious. In fact it was difficult for a time to ascertain whether or not he was alive. More water was brought from the spring and Mr. Cook and Riley continued to minister to the sufferer. Some of the worst of his burns were bound up with strips of shirts offered by members of the party, and his outer clothing was removed. As a matter of fact a large portion of it was so burned that it crumbled to powder at a mere touch.

"He's alive," said Sergeant Riley after a few moments.

"Then he ought to recover," exclaimed Mr. Cook. "That is, unless he has inhaled some of the flames and injured his lungs in some way."

"Only a doctor can tell that," said the sergeant. "Whether he gets well or not, one thing is certain and that is he'll be in the hospital a long time."

"That's right," agreed Mr. Cook. "I wish he could talk though."

At that moment Bob arrived with the automobile and presently Mr. Wernberg was lifted into the tonneau and a blanket wrapped around him. He was still unconscious, but his face was drawn with pain that fortunately he could not feel. Much as the men who cared for him despised him for his suspected work with the gang of spies and plotters they could only feel pity for his sufferings.

Mr. Cook, Hugh, and Sergeant Riley accompanied Bob on his trip to the High Ridge Hospital, and the three other members of the party were left to watch the fire and see that it did not spread, and then they were to follow in the other car. Donovan the detective seemed to be himself once more and related briefly the story of how he had rescued Mr. Wernberg.

"I rushed into the house," he said, "and as I stuck my head inside the door a wave of smoke caught me full in the face. At first I expected I should have to turn back, but I kept on and presently the air cleared for a minute. I knew the trapped man was on the second floor so I hurried around looking for the stairs. Finally I found them and though they were awfully rickety I got up.

"The smoke seemed to be thicker on the second floor and I could scarcely see. I heard a cry and followed it, stumbling and falling along the hall. The door of one big room was smashed and the smoke poured out of there as if it was a chimney. No one was in that room and I came out into the hall again. I heard another call, and traced it as coming from a room where the door was closed. I grabbed the door-knob, but it was locked. 'Help! Help!' I heard from inside. 'Unlock the door!' I shouted. 'I have no key,' said the voice, so I put my shoulder to the door and tried to force it.

"I was choking and coughing and gasping, what with the smoke and all, and it was hard work standing there. I shoved with all my might though, and all of a sudden the door gave way. I went shooting into the room and fell right over a man stretched out on the floor. 'They blew me up,' he cried and fainted. Well, the room was full of smoke and all around the edges little tongues of flame were playing; the fellow had fallen to the floor and been terribly burned. I picked him up and staggered out with him and you know the rest."

Donovan himself was badly burned about his hands

and face. Every one knows how painful is a burn, but the detective made no complaint, in spite of the fact that he must have been suffering agonies.

Meanwhile Bob was speeding the car back towards High Ridge. He broke all speed laws on the way, but he had been warned that haste was imperative if Mr. Wernberg's life was to be saved. Besides he had a police officer in the car with him and knew that he was safe.

In an incredibly short time he pulled up in front of the hospital. Two orderlies were summoned, and soon Mr. Wernberg, placed on a stretcher, was being carried into the building. Once or twice his eyelids fluttered as though he were about to regain consciousness, but he did not seem to possess sufficient strength to accomplish that end.

Two doctors hastily took him in charge, Sergeant Riley left word that he should be summoned the instant the patient was able to talk, and then Bob ran the car around to police headquarters. Sergeant Riley invited them all into his office and they discussed what their next move should be.

A band passed by the door, several men in uniform followed behind on their way to the city square where they were to make speeches in order to urge more enlistments in the army and navy. Crowds of enthusiastic people trailed the procession, and Bob could not help wondering if the people realized that danger threatened the country from within as well as from without.

Presently the car bearing the three detectives arrived at

Paul G. Tomlinson

headquarters. They reported that nearby farmers had come to the scene of the fire, which was now in such condition that no harm could come from it. The farmers had promised to watch over the smouldering ruins, for ruins were now all that remained of the old house.

Donovan once again related his story and then went off in search of a doctor to care for his burns.

"It's bad business, Sergeant," said Mr. Cook.

"It is," Riley agreed. "I'd like to get me hands on some of them fellows."

"Seems queer that they should have blown up one of their own men."

"'Twas probably a mistake. Perhaps they saw us coming and were in such a hurry that our friend Wernberg had no time to get away."

"But look here," protested Bob. "Don't you remember what Donovan said that Mr. Wernberg said when he burst into the room?"

"He said, 'they tried to blow me up,'" quoted Mr. Cook.

"Exactly," exclaimed Bob. "Doesn't that seem queer to you?"

"He was probably left there by mistake, as the sergeant says," said Mr. Cook.

"But," Bob insisted, "the door was locked."

The men looked at one another blankly.

"I had forgotten that," said Sergeant Riley.

"Well," insisted Bob, "I'd like to have that part of it explained to me. You don't suppose for a minute that Mr. Wernberg locked himself in, do you?"

"I shouldn't think he would," Mr. Cook admitted. "But if he didn't do it, who did? That's what I'd like to know."

"Mr. Wernberg wasn't the only man in the house, you know," said Bob.

"Who else was there?"

"Didn't Hugh and two of the detectives chase another man?"

"Yez mean the fake detective?" asked Sergeant Riley.

"I do."

"But wasn't he in the same gang? What use would it be to him to blow up one of his own men?"

"I don't know," said Bob. "Still I don't believe that Mr. Wernberg locked himself in and threw the key out of the window."

"Doesn't sound likely," the sergeant agreed. "I'd like to know why those two men were enemies though. From all I can learn I should think they were working for the same purpose. Why should that fake detective be so eager to get that paper away from yez, and to get you boys away if he wasn't up to something suspicious?"

"Don't ask me," exclaimed Bob. "It's too deep for me, and I get more and more mixed up all the time."

"Well, I believe it's just as I said," continued Riley. "They were both parts of the same crowd. There must have been evidence against them in that house and they wanted to destroy it. Your fake detective blew it up and Mr. Wernberg got caught in there by mistake."

"How do you explain the locked door?" asked Bob.

"I don't, but there must be some explanation for it."

"You think it was an accident, don't you?"

"I do," said Sergeant Riley firmly. "When Mr. Wernberg gets so he can talk I'll bet he'll say the same thing."

Bob merely shrugged his shoulders. He did not think that the sergeant's explanation was correct, but he could offer no better one himself so he said nothing. After all it might be that in the hurry to get away there was a mix up and Mr. Wernberg was left behind, locked in the room. Bob had no doubt in his mind that Mr. Wernberg was a member of a gang that was plotting against the United States. In his heart he felt sure he was guilty.

On the other hand if the fake detective was not equally guilty he would be surprised. Certainly no man would disguise himself in that way who had honorable motives. Nor would any man run away as he had done, or fire a pistol at real officers of the law unless he was engaged in some evil doing.

How were these two men connected? That was the question that bothered Bob. He felt that there was some connection between them, and yet why should one of them be locked in the second story of a house while the other one put a bomb under it and burned it up? Perhaps after all it was as Sergeant Riley had suggested.

"Come on, boys; we'll go home," exclaimed Mr. Cook.

"Thank yez for coming with us," said Sergeant Riley, as Mr. Cook and the two boys rose to their feet preparatory to leaving.

"Not at all," said Mr. Cook cordially. "If there is anything further we can do to help, please call on us."

"I will," said the sergeant. "Thank yez again."

"And don't forget to let us know what Mr. Wernberg has to say."

"I won't."

They went out and got into the automobile and a few moments later were home again.

"After you put away the car, I want you to take a note down to the Wernbergs for me," said Mr. Cook to Bob as he mounted the steps of the house.

"To tell them what happened to Mr. Wernberg?"

"Yes."

"I should think it would be better to go and see them."

"No doubt it would, but somehow I don't like the idea of having to go and talk to Mrs. Wernberg about it. I suppose I'm a coward."

"I don't blame you," exclaimed Bob, and after he had returned the car to its place in the garage he came back to the house to wait until his father should have finished the note he was writing.

When it was ready Mr. Cook handed it to Bob, who at once started for the Wernbergs' house, accompanied by Hugh. They discussed the recent turn of events in the mystery and were somewhat at a loss as to what their next move should be. Now that the old deserted house was a thing of the past they did not know where to look for the seat of the conspiracy. They did decide, however, that in so far as it was possible they would keep watch on number twelve eighty-two Elm Street.

They mounted the front steps of the Wernbergs' house, and Bob advanced toward the door bell. Before he rang it, however, he spied an envelope lying at his feet, half concealed under the door mat. He stooped to pick it up, and as he glanced at it he uttered an exclamation of surprise.

"Look, Hugh," he exclaimed.

The envelope was of plain white paper and addressed to Mr. Wernberg. There was no street number on it, merely the name. This in itself was not particularly odd, nor was it the cause of Bob's surprise. On the other side of the envelope, however, was scrawled a drawing. It was the picture of an alligator.

CHAPTER XVII

A MESSAGE

"Well, Hugh, what do you think about that?" demanded Bob.

Hugh looked blankly at the rude drawing on the back of the envelope. "I don't know," he said slowly. "Why should they send Mr. Wernberg one of these?"

"Unless it's a message from one member of the gang to another."

"But Mr. Wernberg is in the hospital."

"The others may not know that."

"That's true," Hugh agreed. "This handwriting is the same as that on the messages that came to your father and to Heinrich too."

"I know it, and the same as in the list we found in the old house."

"What do you suppose the alligator stands for?"

"I've no idea. Why did they steal Percy?"

Paul G. Tomlinson

"Anyway we'd better ring the bell and deliver our message. We can't stand out here on the porch all day, you know."

Bob pushed the electric bell, and almost instantly the front door was opened by Frank Wernberg. It would seem as if he had been behind the door waiting all the time. His close-cropped light hair bristled fiercely, and his nose was still slightly swollen; his chin also was still raw where Bob had planted his fist the day before. Bob thought how much longer ago than that it seemed; so many things had happened in the last two days.

"What are you doing here?" demanded Frank brusquely.

Bob and Hugh had been so surprised by the sudden opening of the door that for a moment neither one of them replied.

"What do you want?" exclaimed Frank.

"We've got a letter for your mother," said Bob.

Frank glared at them under lowering brows. "Who from?" he asked.

"That's for her to find out," said Bob. "It's addressed to her you see."

Frank snatched the letter from Bob's outstretched hand, and made as if he was about to go in and shut the door.

"Wait a minute," exclaimed Hugh. "Here's another."

"What kind of a joke are you trying to play on me?"

cried Frank angrily.

"None at all," said Hugh. "This one is for your father."

Frank grew red in the face, "If this is a joke I swear you'll be sorry for it," he exclaimed hotly.

"It's no joke at all," said Hugh. "We found this letter lying here under the mat. I was just going to hand it to you."

Frank took the letter from Hugh and looked at it suspiciously. Then he turned it over and looked at the back of it. Suddenly he turned pale.

Bob and Hugh, watching him closely, noticed this fact, and Bob, suddenly plucking up courage, determined to speak of it.

"What does that alligator mean, Frank?" he asked.

The color rushed back into Frank's face. He looked as though he were going to run. He swallowed hard two or three times, choked, and then swallowed again. "I don't know," he blurted out finally, and stepping inside slammed the door shut in the faces of the two boys.

Hugh looked at Bob and smiled. "Frank was certainly glad to see us, wasn't he?" he said sarcastically.

"I should say so," Bob agreed. "Let's go home."

They went down the steps and walked slowly in the direction of the Cook home.

"Frank's a queer fellow," said Hugh finally.

"He certainly is," Bob agreed.

"Do you think he knows what has happened to his father?"

"I doubt it. I don't believe he would have been so surly if he had known."

"What do you think about the alligator?"

"I'm sure I don't know," said Bob. "It must mean something though, and Frank must know what it is. Did you see how pale he got when he saw it!"

"Maybe it's the sign of some secret society like the Black Hand, or the Ku Klux Klan, or something like that."

"Still I can't understand why they should send a warning to Mr. Wernberg if he is a member of the gang."

"It may not have been a warning," said Hugh. "Perhaps it was just a message of some kind or another."

"Then why should Frank have been so scared when he saw it?"

"Don't ask me. I'm getting more mixed up every minute."

They turned into the Cooks' yard and slowly approached the house. A man and woman were just disappearing around the corner.

"Who are they?" Hugh inquired.

"Lena, the cook, and one of her beaux," said Bob.

"I thought Heinrich was in love with her."

"He is," laughed Bob, "but he has a rival, and that's the man."

"What's his name?"

"Karl Hoffmann."

"Another German," said Hugh soberly.

"Say, Hugh," laughed Bob, "you certainly are suspicious. You suspect good old Lena, and now you suspect the man with her because he has a German name. Why, that man Hoffmann has worked for father for years, and father thinks the world of him."

"That doesn't mean he may not be mistaken," Hugh insisted.

"Why, father has even selected him as one of the guards for the factory," said Bob. "I guess that shows how much confidence he has in him."

"But suppose Lena is disloyal," exclaimed Hugh. "If Karl Hoffmann is in love with her there's no telling what she might get him to do."

"But Lena is not disloyal," said Bob peevishly. He was becoming tired of Hugh's constant slurs against the people whom his father employed.

"Well, I'd watch them all," said Hugh.

Bob offered no further comment. He could not convince Hugh that his suspicions were unfounded so he decided there could be no use in arguing with him. They entered the house and found Mr. Cook seated in the library alone.

"Did you deliver my note?" he asked.

"We did," replied Bob.

"Who came to the door?"

"Frank," and Bob related their experiences to his father. Mr. Cook was much interested and puzzled by the manner in which Frank had acted when he saw the drawing of the alligator on the back of the envelope.

"We thought perhaps it might be the sign of some secret society," said Hugh.

"Possibly so," agreed Mr. Cook. "Let's see; the same sign was on the paper you found in the old house, Heinrich got a note with the picture on it, and now this letter you picked up on the Wernbergs' porch had it too."

"And the handwriting was the same as on that postal card you got this morning," said Bob.

"I didn't see any picture on that though."

"No," agreed Bob. "Neither did I."

"I threw the card away," said Mr. Cook. "I was afraid your mother might find it and worry."

"Perhaps there won't be any more trouble, now that Mr. Wernberg is out of the way," suggested Bob. "If he was the leader of the gang, his burns will keep him in the hospital and out of mischief for some time to come."

"You didn't hear what happened this afternoon then?" asked his father.

"No, what?" demanded Bob and Hugh in one breath.

"You remember the railroad bridge, don't you?"

"I guess we'll never forget that, will we, Hugh?" exclaimed Bob. "You don't mean that they tried to blow it up again?"

"Well, it looks so," said Mr. Cook. "One of the guards on the bridge this afternoon saw a man coming down the river in a rowboat. He called to him to halt, but the man kept right on. The guard challenged him three times, but as the man gave no answer he fired at him."

"Did he kill him?" demanded Bob excitedly.

"No," said Mr. Cook, "he didn't try to kill him. He just wanted to scare him, and when he fired the man jumped out of the boat into the water. The guard hurried down to the bank of the river, but the man had scrambled ashore and run off; you know it's quite a long distance from where the railroad tracks cross the bridge down to the water. The guard got a long pole and waded out into the river after the boat. He caught it finally and when he had hauled it ashore he found it was loaded with dynamite. Of course no one knows, but they think he planned to blow up the bridge."

"Whew!" exclaimed Hugh. "The man got away, you say?"

"Yes, unfortunately."

"Couldn't the guard see what he looked like?"

"Yes, he did see that, and here is the interesting part."

"What do you mean?"

"Why," said Mr. Cook, "the man was rather slight, weighing perhaps a hundred and fifty pounds and he had a close-cropped black mustache."

"The fake detective!" exclaimed Bob. "Was that who it was?"

"The description fits him, doesn't it?"

"Yes," agreed Hugh, "but he was out at the old house this afternoon. How could he be on the river at the same time?"

"He was out at the old house early this afternoon," said Mr. Cook. "This episode at the bridge happened only about an hour ago."

"He must have hurried right down there," exclaimed Bob. "When he realized that the police were on his trail he probably decided he had no time to lose, and that's why he dared try such a thing in broad daylight."

"Where did you hear about it, Mr. Cook?" inquired Hugh.

"Sergeant Riley just told me over the telephone; I had called him up to inquire how Mr. Wernberg was getting along."

"How is he?" asked Bob.

"Pretty bad yet; once in a while he recovers consciousness, but only for a few minutes. Besides he suffers so from his burns he can't do any talking."

"And meanwhile his gang keeps on working," said Hugh.

"Is that fake detective part of his gang?" said Bob. "He's the one who blew him up."

"I don't know," exclaimed Hugh in despair. "We just go 'round and 'round in circles and don't seem to get anywhere at all."

"But the fact remains, doesn't it, boys," inquired Mr. Cook, "that whether we know who the gang is, and what the relations are between the two gangs - if there are two - that somebody is hard at work plotting against this country? Also they are becoming bolder for they know that their time is short; sooner or later they are bound to be caught."

"You're afraid for your factory to-night, aren't you, father?" asked Bob.

"I am, indeed," said Mr. Cook.

Bob was on the point of asking if he and Hugh might not help guard it when the telephone rang and his father was called away to answer it.

CHAPTER XVIII

KARL HOFFMANN

"Let's go down and talk to Heinrich," exclaimed Bob when his father left the room.

"Aren't you going to ask your father if we can stand guard to-night?"

"Wait till after dinner. I'll ask him then."

"Do you think he'll let us?"

"I guess so. It depends on how badly he needs us."

They went out, and just at the corner of the porch met Karl Hoffmann. He had said good-by to Lena and was on his way home. Bob knew him well, as he did most of his father's employees, for much of his spare time was spent down at the factory. Furthermore, on account of Lena, Hoffmann was a frequent visitor in the Cook home.

He was a big, fine looking fellow of about forty. He had black hair and a piercing black eye, a typical Prussian, for it was from that province in Germany that his parents had migrated some twenty-five years previously. He was a powerful man, standing nearly six feet in height, and not yet showing any tendency towards stoutness, so common among Germans.

"Hello, Karl," cried Bob cheerily.

Hoffmann stopped short. His face had been drawn into a scowl as he strode along, and he had been deeply engrossed in his own thoughts. Bob had often seen him that way after talking with Lena, however. She was something of a flirt and received lightly her admirers' advances. Many a time both Heinrich and Karl had been driven almost to desperation by the manner in which she treated them. Neither did they like each other, because they were rivals.

"Hello there, Bob," he exclaimed, his face brightening. Bob had always been a marked favorite of his, and many a thing he had showed him about the machinery at the factory.

"You look mad," said Bob.

"I was sort of mad," said Karl. "I was worried."

"Anything I can do for you?" Bob inquired, nudging Hugh with his elbow. He loved to tease both Karl and Heinrich about their love affair.

"No, thanks," replied Karl seriously. "It will be all right I hope."

"I hear you're making ammunition down at the factory," said Bob.

"Yes."

"Keeps you pretty busy, doesn't it?"

"It certainly does. We're going to work both a night and day shift next week."

"You want to watch out for some of these bomb plotters," said Bob. "There are a lot of them around here, I understand."

"That so?" exclaimed Karl. "I hadn't heard of any."

"Well, they're here all right."

"We have the plant guarded, you know."

"I know it. It's a good thing too."

"I think it's unnecessary," said Karl. "I told your father so, too."

"You're more of an optimist than he is, I guess," laughed Bob. "He's heard a lot of things that have made him sort of nervous."

"That so?" demanded Karl. "I wonder what they were?"

"I don't know," Bob lied. He thought that if his father wanted to tell his employees any details he would probably do so himself.

Just then Hugh plucked his sleeve. "Look, Bob," he exclaimed. "Here comes Frank in to see you."

Bob swung around just in time to see Frank Wernberg on a bicycle turning into the driveway. He rode a few yards and then suddenly turned around and rode out again. Coming to the street once more he dismounted from his bicycle, and gazed back at the Cooks' house as if he was debating whether he should go in or not. Finally, however, he seemed to decide against that course and jumping on his wheel rode off down the street.

"He lost his nerve," exclaimed Hugh. "You ought to have called to him."

"A fine chance of that," snorted Bob. "If he wants to he can come in here and see me, but I won't run after him."

"Who was that boy?" asked Karl curiously.

"Frank Wernberg," said Bob.

"Wernberg?" exclaimed Karl. "Does his father live down on the corner here?"

"Yes."

"I don't like that man," said Karl soberly. "I hope he's not a friend of yours."

"He is not," exclaimed Bob warmly. "What do you know about him, Karl?"

"Nothing much; I just don't trust him."

"No one seems to like him," laughed Bob. "I guess he won't bother us for some time to come though now."

"Why not?" demanded Karl quickly.

"He's sick."

"What's the matter with him?"

"I don't know," said Bob evasively. He suddenly remembered that probably he had no right to talk about what they had done that day. "All I know is that he's in the hospital."

"Serves him right," exclaimed Karl. "That's a good place for him and for all of his same kind."

If Hugh had had any lingering doubts as to whether or not Karl was loyal they were now dissipated. If Mr. Wernberg was implicated in German plots against the United States, certainly no man who sympathized with him would hate him as Karl Hoffmann plainly did.

"We may come down and help you guard the factory to-night, Karl," said Bob. "You'll be there, won't you?"

"Yes, I'll be there," said Karl. "I wish you wouldn't come though."

"Why not!"

"Suppose something should happen and you got hurt?"

"I thought you said there was no danger."

"I don't think there is, but I know your father doesn't agree with me, and if something should happen to you, just think how badly he'd feel."

"We want to help though," insisted Bob.

"Let the men who are paid for it do the guarding."

"But it's my father's plant," said Bob. "You don't think I want anything to happen to it if I can help it, do you?"

"If he wants you to come, all right," said Karl. "Still you take my advice and stay home."

He said good-by to the boys and went off toward his house. He had to be at the factory early and wanted his supper before he went on duty.

"Well, Hugh?" demanded Bob after Karl had gone. "What do you think of him?"

"Oh, he's all right," said Hugh.

"Do you think he would be disloyal?"

"No, I guess any man who hates Mr. Wernberg as much as he does can't be pro-German. Still he was funny about not wanting us at the factory to-night."

"I know why that was," exclaimed Bob. "He thinks we're just a couple of kids and would only be in everybody's way."

"I guess so," Hugh agreed. "He seemed like a nice fellow all right."

"He is, but Heinie doesn't think so. Let's go ask him about Karl now, and I'll guarantee you'll see some fun. Heinie gets mad the minute you mention his name."

"He's jealous of him, isn't he?"

"He surely is. Lena likes Karl better than she does him, I think, and I guess Heinie knows it. That's why he doesn't like Karl."

"Still I don't blame Lena," observed Hugh. "Karl is certainly better looking."

They found Heinrich seated on a chair in the garage busily counting over a large pile of bills. When the boys appeared he showed the same embarrassment he had when Bob had surprised him at the same work before.

"The rich man again," laughed Bob, but Heinrich said nothing.

"Any trace of Percy?" Bob inquired.

"No," said Heinrich sorrowfully. "I guess he iss gone."

"We've just been talking to Karl Hoffmann," said Bob. "You don't suppose he could have stolen him, do you?"

Immediately Heinrich's manner changed. He rose to his feet angrily, while Bob nudged Hugh. Heinrich became pale with rage.

"That scoundrel!" he stammered. "I would not be surprised if he would steal poor Percy. He iss mean and low enough to do anything."

"Why, Heinie," said Bob mildly. "I always thought Karl was a fine fellow."

"He iss a low down snake!" cried Heinrich. "I would not trust that fellow mit two cents."

"Lena likes him," said Bob.

Heinrich became madder than before at this remark. He stuttered with rage, and advancing toward Bob shook his clenched fist in his face. "Sure she like him," he cried. "Why not? He gives her presents all the time and it iss for that that she like him. She knows what a low down cur he iss, for I have told her so. Only because he has money and can give her presents does she like him. But I will show her!"

"What are you going to do?" demanded Bob, somewhat alarmed by the violence of Heinrich's manner.

"I buy her presents now," exclaimed Heinrich. "You see that?" he demanded, pulling the roll of bills out of his pocket. "You see that?" he repeated. "Well, I got some money now, and I show her who can buy nice presents. She like me better than Hoffmann when I get more money than he." Heinrich looked at the bills held in his fist, and then jammed them back fiercely into his pocket.

"Where'd you get all the money?" asked Bob. "You didn't draw it out of the savings bank, did you?"

"No," exclaimed Heinrich. "I earn it."

"Working for father?"

"No, for Mr. Wernberg."

"What!" exclaimed Bob, completely taken by surprise. He and Hugh looked at each other in astonishment. This was a new turn of events.

"Yes," said Heinrich. "I do some work for Mr. Wernberg; he iss a fine man too."

"What was the work?" inquired Bob. He remembered that Hugh had advised him to watch their chauffeur. He never imagined, however, that even if Heinrich was guilty he would be so bold as to confess brazenly that he was employed by a man to plot against the United States. Still, he had always suspected that poor Heinrich was not quite right in his head.

"I cannot say," said Heinrich. "The work iss secret."

"Why, Heinie," exclaimed Bob. "I never thought you would do a thing like that."

"Why not?" demanded Heinrich. "I do my work here, don't I? Why should I not make a little extra money if I can?"

"But Mr. Wernberg is a bad man."

"He iss not," Heinrich protested stoutly. "He iss one man who knows right from wrong."

Bob shook his head sorrowfully. It hurt him to discover that their chauffeur, a man he had grown up with and liked, was working hand in glove with Mr. Wernberg. He never would have believed it possible had he not heard it with his own ears from Heinrich himself. It was a great shock to him and he knew how badly his father and mother would feel. Of course he must tell his father.

CHAPTER XIX

A DISCUSSION

"Come on, Hugh, let's go," exclaimed Bob. Heinrich had turned away from them and walked off angrily. The combination of Lena and Karl and Mr. Wernberg, had been too much for him to stand apparently. He was mad clear through.

"Well," said Bob, when they were outside, "I never would have believed that."

"I told you to watch them all," Hugh reminded him.

"I know you did, and I guess you were right. Why poor old Heinie should be such a fool is more than I can understand."

"Are you going to tell your father?"

"I suppose I must."

"Will he tell the police?"

"I don't know. I should think perhaps he'd have to, though."

"It's too bad," murmured Hugh. He knew how fond his

friend was of Heinrich.

"At any rate Karl is all right I guess," said Bob.

"I'll agree with you there," said Hugh. "How about Lena?"

"Don't ask me. I feel as if I couldn't think."

Mr. Cook met them on the front porch and was at once impressed by the expression on the faces of the two boys.

"What's wrong?" he demanded.

"We've just had an awful shock," said Hugh.

"What is it? Tell me, Bob," his father urged.

"Heinrich is one of Mr. Wernberg's gang."

"Say that again," exclaimed Mr. Cook incredulously.

"Heinrich is working with Mr. Wernberg. You ought to see the pile of money he has been paid already."

"Why, Bob," exclaimed Mr. Cook amazedly. "I think you must be mistaken."

"He just told us himself," said Bob. "He said Mr. Wernberg was a fine man and one of the few who knew right from wrong."

"How did he happen to tell you all this?"

Bob related the circumstances to his father. When he

had finished Mr. Cook remained silent for several minutes.

"I am so sorry," he said finally. "I don't see why Heinrich told you."

"He was mad," said Bob, "and jealous."

"A dangerous man to hire for that kind of work I should think," exclaimed Mr. Cook. "If he would say as much as he did to you this afternoon I don't see what there is to prevent him from telling all he knows."

"You mean he might give the whole thing away?"

"Exactly."

"Still," said Bob, "Heinie can be awfully stubborn sometimes."

"I know it. We'd have to be clever to get a full confession from him I imagine."

"I don't see what use he could be to Mr. Wernberg," said Hugh.

"It's a favorite method of these German plotters, Hugh," said Mr. Cook. "Very often they get some simple-minded, ignorant fellow like Heinrich and make a tool of him. Heinrich hasn't got brains enough to think of anything himself."

"Are you going to turn him over to the police?" inquired Bob.

"I was just thinking of that," said Mr. Cook. "I

certainly would hate to do it."

"But he may do some damage."

"I know it and I think I know what I'll do. To-night I expect to be at the factory practically all night; I'll keep Heinrich with me on one pretext or another. He'll be right with me all the time so that he won't be able to do any harm and besides I can watch his actions. I am still hoping that he may prove to be loyal."

"I'm afraid he won't," said Bob.

"I'm afraid not too," agreed his father. "Still I won't let him out of my sight and when morning comes we can decide what ought to be done about Him."

"If it isn't too late."

"Let's hope not," exclaimed Mr. Cook earnestly.

"Hugh and I would like to help guard the factory to-night," said Bob.

"I think we have plenty of guards," said Mr. Cook. "You'd better stay home and go to bed; you've had a busy time of it the last two days."

"I know it, but we want to help," explained Bob. "Somehow I have a feeling that something is going to happen down there to-night."

"Suppose it does, and you get hurt. What would your mother say?"

"That's what Karl Hoffmann said," exclaimed Hugh.

"Karl is usually right too," said Mr. Cook. "He takes so much responsibility about my personal affairs that really I don't know what I'd do without him."

"He was afraid we'd get hurt," sniffed Bob.

"Karl likes you," said his father. "He doesn't want anything to happen to you."

"We can take care of ourselves."

"I know that," his father assented. "Do you want to go very much?"

"We certainly do," cried Bob and Hugh in one breath.

"Well," said Mr. Cook, "I'm proud of you for wanting to help, and under the circumstances I don't see how I can refuse."

"That's great!" cried Bob enthusiastically.

"It won't all be fun by a good deal," his father warned him.

"We know that, but we're ready to do anything that comes along."

The two boys were much excited at the prospect of the guard duty. It seemed to them that at last they had been recognized as capable of aiding in the defense of their country. Perhaps if they had known what awaited them they would not have been quite so enthusiastic.

Paul G. Tomlinson

CHAPTER XX

ANOTHER SUSPECT

Hugh was going home for dinner, and was to return shortly afterward to accompany Bob and his father to the factory. He left the house and Bob started upstairs to prepare himself for the evening meal. On the landing of the stairs he heard some one talking over the telephone and stopped to listen. Of late he had become suspicious of every one and had fallen into the habit of noticing every little thing that happened.

It was the cook's voice and he was doubly interested at once.

"Yes," he heard her say, "this is Lena."

Bob flattened himself against the wall and listened intently.

"What's that?" Lena demanded over the 'phone. "In the hospital, you say!"

There was a pause while the other person talked to her.

"I will try to be there," said Lena. "I also have a message for you, but I don't know whether I should say it now or not; those blamed detectives are on to us."

There ensued another pause while Bob became more and more excited. What was this plot anyway that turned old and trusted servants against their masters? Was no one to be relied upon? Who could be trusted?

"Yes, I will tell Heinrich," said Lena speaking again. "Good-by."

She hung up the receiver and Bob continued up the stairs, whistling and trying to act as if he had heard nothing. He met Lena in the hall and she eyed him narrowly.

"Hello, Lena," he exclaimed cheerfully. "Fine day, isn't it?"

"Yes, Mr. Bob," she said, and passed on toward the back stairs.

No sooner was she gone than Bob turned and sped down stairs again to the library. He burst into the room breathlessly, causing his father, who was reading his evening paper to glance up in surprise.

"Father," exclaimed Bob in a tense whisper, "Lena's in it too."

"What's that?" demanded his father. "Sit down, Bob."

Bob grasped a chair and sat down facing his father. "Lena's in it too," he repeated.

"In what?"

"In the plot with Mr. Wernberg."

Mr. Cook laid down his paper. "Tell me what you know," he said soberly.

Bob repeated the part of Lena's telephone conversation that he had heard. "You see," he exclaimed, "she spoke about the hospital and that must have meant Mr. Wernberg; then she said the detectives were on to them; finally she said she'd tell Heinrich and also try to be there to-night."

"You don't know what she is to tell Heinrich and where she is to be to-night?"

"No, sir," said Bob. "That's all I heard."

"Well," exclaimed Mr. Cook after a moment's pause. "This is a nice state of affairs."

"What are you going to do about it?" asked Bob. "Are you still going to wait until to-morrow before you report Heinie to the police?"

Mr. Cook passed his hand across his brow as if to wipe away the doubts that assailed him. "Heinrich and Lena both," he muttered. "What a pity."

"I tell you what I'll do," he exclaimed finally. "I'll take Heinrich along with me to-night just as I planned, and I'll tell your mother under no conditions to let Lena go out this evening. In the morning we may know better what to do."

"I have a better scheme than that," said Bob eagerly.

"Tell me what it is."

"Take Heinrich along with you and watch him all the time; that part is all right. But let Lena go out if she wants to."

"What's the point of that?" demanded his father. "For all we know Lena may he able to do more harm than Heinrich; certainly she's smarter."

"Let her go out," said Bob, "and I'll go with her."

"I don't see what you mean."

"I'll follow her."

"You'd have to be disguised."

"I know it; I'll attend to that though."

"It might lead you to some very dangerous spot," said Mr. Cook. "I hate to have you do it."

"Look here, father," exclaimed Bob earnestly. "We're at war with Germany, aren't we? Well, just think of all those millions of men over in Europe on the battle-fields; all the English and French, and Italians, and Belgians, and Russians, and all the others. If the United States is in the war we ought to be willing to do our part. Our allies in Europe are fighting for us as much as for themselves, and it seems to me that to disguise myself and follow the cook is a small thing for me to contribute to the common cause."

"I guess you're right, Bob," said his father.

"Why look here," continued Bob. "Just think of the way those men over there are every one of them risking their lives a hundred times a day. We just can't sit still and let them do all our fighting for us. We can give them money and food and I think we ought to expect to give our lives too if it is necessary. I know I don't want to hide behind somebody else and let him fight for me."

"You're all right, my boy," exclaimed Mr. Cook, rising to his feet. He grasped his son affectionately by the arm, and there were tears in his eyes as he did so. "You're all right," he repeated, "and I'm proud of you. You've got the spirit that every true American should have, and which I believe they do have. When Germany finds herself facing a million American troops and sees the Stars and Stripes floating from the opposing trenches she'll know she's beaten. I hope we'll show them that we mean business and the sooner we do, the quicker the war will be over."

"What kind of a disguise can I wear?" asked Bob.

"I guess you won't need a very elaborate one. Isn't there a false-face in the house with whiskers or a mustache on it!"

"I think there is one I used last hallowe'en."

"Get that then," said his father. "We can rip off the whiskers and glue them on your face. Put on an old suit of clothes and a sweater; wear a slouch hat and take along that hickory cane that I have. That ought to fix you up all right."

"I guess it will," exclaimed Bob, much excited at the prospect. "I'll go upstairs and look for the false-face now."

"Don't put it on until after dinner."

"I won't," said Bob as he hurried up to the attic in search of the disguise he was to wear. In a cupboard on the top floor he found the false-face and quickly tore the whiskers and mustache from it. He brought the handful of hair down to his room and hid it in his closet. He selected the oldest suit he owned and placed it on a chair with an old slouch hat he used to wear when he went fishing.

The announcement that dinner was ready put an end to any further preparations for the time being. The meal was a quiet one and there was but little conversation. Mrs. Cook's thoughts were of Harold and she was greatly worried about him; particularly as she did not know where his regiment had been sent. Mr. Cook, although he too was concerned about his elder son, was occupied principally with anxiety as to the plots that seemed to be brewing all about him, and the possible damage to his factory. Bob, needless to say, was highly excited over the prospects of adventure that the evening held forth for him.

Finally dinner was over. Mr. Cook dispatched Bob to the garage with a message to Heinrich to have the car ready in half an hour. As Bob ran across the lawn he met Lena returning from the garage. "Aha," he thought as he greeted her, "you saw Heinrich all right, didn't you?" He was fully convinced now that their cook and chauffeur were agents of Mr. Wernberg, and partners in crime. A moment later he reached the garage.

"Father wants you to bring the car around in half an hour," he announced to Heinrich, who was engaged in putting on a clean collar and necktie.

Paul G. Tomlinson

"What!" exclaimed Heinrich angrily. Bob had never before seen their chauffeur question any order that his father had given. "I can't."

"Those are his orders," said Bob, eyeing Heinrich closely.

"Does he want me to drive him out?"

"He does."

"But I can't," cried Heinrich. "I can't, I tell you; I have an appointment."

"I guess you'll have to break it then," was Bob's retort.

Heinrich wrung his hands in desperation. "What shall I do?" he moaned. "What shall I do?"

"Can't you change your appointment?"

"I do not think so," wailed Heinrich. "This iss terrible. Do you think your father would change his mind if I should speak to him?"

"I'm sure he wouldn't," said Bob. "I know he wants the car and he wants you to drive it. I heard him say that positively."

"This iss terrible," repeated Heinrich. "What will they do mitout me?"

"Who?"

"My friends."

"It's too bad," said Bob, more convinced every moment that mischief was afoot that evening. "I don't know what you can do about it though."

"Of course I have to go mit your father," said Heinrich finally, heaving a great sigh. "I wonder if he will want the car for long."

"I think he will."

"Very well," said Heinrich, becoming resigned to his fate, "I will be there but only because I do not wish to lose my job. But I fear something will happen."

"That's just what we want to prevent," thought Bob grimly. "All right then, Heinie," he said aloud. "Father will expect you in half an hour."

He hurried back to the house, warned his father that he should keep Heinrich always within sight, and related his conversation with the chauffeur as an argument for this course. Then he went upstairs, two steps at a time to make ready his disguise. While he was there Hugh arrived and went up to Bob's room.

"What are you doing, Bob?" he demanded.

"Putting on a disguise."

"What for?"

Bob told him.

"I want to go with you," exclaimed Hugh eagerly. "Two would be better than one anyway."

"Where are you going to get a disguise?"

"I'll borrow part of yours. You can certainly spare enough of those whiskers to make me a mustache anyway."

"You ought to have another hat."

"You can lend me an old cap, can't you? I've got on the oldest suit I own."

Bob brought out the glue pot and with Hugh's assistance was soon adorned with a set of black whiskers and a mustache. His hair did not match at all, but as he expected to wear a hat pulled far down over his eyes that fact did not make much difference. He put on the hat, and wearing his old clothes and a sweater looked at himself in the mirror.

"Whew," he exclaimed, "I'm certainly a hard looking character."

"You certainly are," agreed Hugh, "and you look about forty years old."

"All the better," said Bob. "Now let's get you fixed up."

With what was left of Bob's whiskers a small black mustache was twisted into shape and glued to Hugh's upper lip. It was remarkable to see what a great change in his appearance it made.

"When we take these things off, all the skin on our faces will come too," said Hugh inspecting himself in the mirror.

"Don't you care," exclaimed Bob. "What we're interested in at present is to have them stay on to-night. How about a hat for you now?" He rummaged around on the closet shelf and produced an old cap and a derby.

"Put the derby on, Hugh," he urged. "You'll look just like Charlie Chaplin."

"That wouldn't do, I'm afraid," laughed Hugh. "I'd have too big a crowd following me."

"Turn up the ends of your mustache and you'll look like the kaiser."

"Not for me!" exclaimed Hugh hastily. "I don't want to look like anything German. I'll wear the cap, I guess. I think that's better than the derby."

At that moment Mr. Cook appeared upon the scene. He stood and looked at the two boys approvingly. "Well," he said, "you certainly look like a couple of tough customers all right. I'm glad you're going along, Hugh; I think two will be better than one."

"Is Lena still here?" asked Bob.

"Still here," said his father. "She's getting ready to leave though and you two had better be prepared."

"Where's Heinrich?"

"He's due in about five minutes."

"You'd better watch him, father," warned Bob.

"Don't worry about that," said Mr. Cook soberly. "I suppose that you two 'things' will come to the factory later. I expect to be there all night."

"We'll try to get there," said Bob. "We'll keep track of Lena as long as we can, and if it's possible we'll report to you at the office."

"Good," exclaimed Mr. Cook. "Don't forget to be very careful, and don't get into trouble if you can help it."

"We'll do our best," Bob promised.

CHAPTER XXI

ON THE STREET

As Mr. Cook left the room the two boys heard the automobile come up the driveway and stop in front of the house. Mrs. Cook and Louise were to spend the evening with an aunt of Bob's a short distance down the street, and Mr. Cook was to take them there in the car. Bob and Hugh waited until they should all leave for they did not want to be seen by any one in their disguises.

Presently they heard the car start off and they knew the coast was clear. Silently they slipped down stairs and out the front door. By the side of the house they paused for a consultation.

"These whiskers itch awfully," exclaimed Bob.

"So does this mustache," said Hugh. "I guess we'll have to endure it though."

"Where shall we wait?"

"Won't Lena come out the back door?"

"I guess so. At any rate she'll have to come around and go down the front walk, there's no other way for her to

Paul G. Tomlinson

get out of the yard."

"Let's cross the street and wait there then."

They followed that plan and presently were standing side by side in the shadow of a tree on the opposite side of the street. Lena could be expected to appear at any minute and they kept a sharp lookout for her.

"What do you suppose is ahead of us to-night?" asked Hugh in a low tone.

"I wish I knew."

"I hope we aren't going off on a wild goose chase."

"You've been saying right along that we ought to watch Lena," Bob reminded his friend.

"I know that and I think it's a good plan. All I say is that she may fool us in some way if we're not careful."

"How do you suppose Mr. Wernberg's getting along in the hospital?"

"I don't know," said Hugh. "I must say though that I'm more interested in Lena."

"I'd like to see our old friend, the false detective."

"So would I. What do you suppose he is -"

"Ssh," hissed Bob suddenly.

Around the corner of the Cooks' house came a woman. She walked briskly and a moment later had reached the street. She gazed apprehensively up and down while the two boys shrank farther back into the shadow; then she started off in the direction of the city's business district.

"That's Lena," whispered Bob. "Come on."

On the opposite side of the street and perhaps a hundred paces in back of the hurrying woman the two boys followed.

"We'll have to keep closer than this when she gets down town," whispered Hugh.

"I know it," agreed Bob. "She'd get suspicious now though."

Now and again Lena stopped and glanced behind her. Every time she did so the boys stopped too; evidently she was afraid of being followed. They met few people and those who did pass them apparently took them for a couple of tramps, for they paid no particular attention to them.

A little distance down the street Lena turned the corner to her right. The two boys as a consequence had to run in order not to lose sight of her. They were fearful lest she should slip away from them and therefore were greatly relieved when they came to the turn and saw her still in front of them.

A few moments later she turned again, and then presently, turned still a third time.

"She's trying to lose us," whispered Bob.

"Maybe not," said Hugh. "This is Elm Street."

"Where's twelve eighty-two!"

"On the next block."

The white stucco house was on the same side of the street with the boys, and as Lena came opposite it she crossed over. Bob and Hugh stopped short under a large maple tree whose trunk cast a shadow affording ample protection from a nearby arclight. From this vantage point they watched the woman they were trailing.

"She's going in," whispered Bob, clutching Hugh's arm excitedly.

Lena turned in from the side walk and started toward the steps of the white stucco house, number twelve eighty-two. Half-way up she paused irresolutely. She acted as if she was puzzled as to what she should do; finally she turned, descended the steps rapidly and continued on down the street.

"That was queer," whispered Bob.

"It looked as though she lost her nerve."

"Why should she be scared to go in where her gang is!"

"Don't ask me. Come on."

Once again they took up the chase. Lena seemed to walk more swiftly than ever now, and it was not an easy task to keep pace with her and still not be seen.

The night was dark with low-hanging clouds, the street lamps affording the only light available. Ahead they could see the reflection from the lights of the main street of the city.

"Do you suppose she dropped a note or anything on that porch back there?" demanded Hugh suddenly.

"I didn't see her do anything like that," said Bob.

"Nor I. At any rate I guess the best thing we can do is to stick close to her."

"Yes, and we'd better keep closer too, now that we are coming to where the stores are. We'll lose track of her if we don't."

"Do you suppose any one will notice that we're disguised?"

"I hope not. There's usually a big crowd on the streets Saturday night though."

"We'll hope for luck," said Hugh earnestly.

They quickened their paces until they were scarcely more than seventy-five feet in back of Lena. There were many people passing them in both directions now, and apparently Lena was not as suspicious as she had been; she glanced behind her no more.

Presently they turned into the main street. The sidewalks were thronged with people and everything was lighted up brilliantly in the glare of arclights and shop windows. Lena was just ahead of the boys and it was not an easy task to follow her in the crowd.

Music sounded down the street. A troop of cavalry was approaching and every one lined the curb to see them pass. Lena stopped and the boys took their places directly behind her. Every trooper was mounted on a coal black horse, and they made a fine showing as they drew near; the crowd began to cheer and many waved small American flags that they were carrying. Women waved their handkerchiefs as the horsemen passed, and much to both Bob's and Hugh's surprise Lena waved her handkerchief and clapped her hands with the others.

"What do you think of that?" whispered Bob.

"Bluff," said Hugh. "She's clever."

The crowd began to break up and presently was moving up and down the street again. Lena started on her way once more, and almost at her heels followed Bob and Hugh. They were beginning to wonder whether they were following a false clue. It might be that Lena had dropped a message on the porch of the house on Elm Street, and if so her work was probably done and there could be no object in following her farther.

Suddenly Hugh seized Bob by the arm. "Look at this man coming," he hissed.

Not thirty feet distant and walking directly toward them was the false detective. There could be no mistaking him. Bob and Hugh, forgetting for the moment that they were disguised were fearful lest he should recognize them as well. A moment later, however, an interesting event happened right before their eyes, and they forgot all else.

As the "detective," the man with whom they had fought that morning, the man who had blown up the deserted house, and whom they suspected of having tried to blow up the railroad bridge in the afternoon, passed Lena he held a slip of paper in his left hand. As she went by she took it with her left hand, though as far as the boys could see the two conspirators had not even looked at each other.

Lena continued on down the street as if nothing had happened, while the detective also kept on as though unconscious of having seen Lena at all. He passed the two boys without even a glance.

Bob and Hugh stopped short.

"What do you think of that?" demanded Hugh. "What'll we do?"

"Follow them," said Bob quickly. "You follow him and I'll trail Lena."

Without another word the two boys separated.

Paul G. Tomlinson

CHAPTER XXII

BOB ACTS QUICKLY

Bob had almost lost sight of Lena through this temporary delay and he hurried ahead through the crowd, bumping into several people, and drawing black looks from many for his rudeness. He was in a hurry, however. He had to catch up with Lena, and there was no time to be polite.

Lena too was hurrying. She threaded her way in and out among the throngs of people, and Bob was hard put to it to keep pace with her. As he rushed along he became more and more puzzled and confused as to what was taking place. There was no doubt in his mind that Lena and Heinrich were working in the interests of Mr. Wernberg and therefore were to be watched closely. Apparently Lena was in league with the fake detective too, else why should he stealthily slip a communication into her hand?

But the detective had blown up the house when Mr. Wernberg was within it and had nearly caused his death. If they were all working together how was that fact to be reconciled with what had befallen him? Probably Mr. Wernberg had been injured accidentally as Sergeant Riley had explained. At all events Lena was hurrying along through the crowd and Bob's task was to follow her. His father was watching Heinrich and it would never do for Bob to let his quarry escape him.

Lena followed the main street for several squares. The crowd was still thick, but Bob kept his eyes on her. Presently she turned down a side street, where it was easier to follow her and Bob heaved a sigh of relief. He was sure he could keep track of her now, and his mind was easier. They passed fewer people all the time, and now the only illuminations were the street lamps and an occasional arclight.

Bob dropped further behind. His one wish was to avert suspicion on Lena's part, and the sight of a tough-looking man with heavy black whiskers, old clothes, and a dilapidated slouch hat dogging her footsteps might well have made her uneasy.

Every hundred feet or so Lena cast a quick glance over her shoulder. Bob did not walk on the stone pavement, but skulked along in the shadow of the hedges and fences except when a passerby came along. Consequently whenever Lena looked behind her he stood still. It was exciting work.

A half-mile or so down the street Lena stopped. She stood under one of the street lamps, and after a sharp glance in all directions, stealthily drew a piece of paper out of the bag she carried. She was plainly nervous, and Bob watched her intently. She was about to read the note that the fake detective had handed to her.

It took Bob only a second to make up his mind. The occasion called for quick action and he acted quickly. Running swiftly and silently on the moist earth, he stole up behind Lena. She was standing still, deeply engrossed in what she read on the paper she held in her hand. Consequently she was unaware of Bob bearing down upon her.

When he was about ten feet behind her, Bob suddenly dashed forward, even more swiftly than before, and before the startled cook knew what was happening he had snatched the paper from her hand and was speeding away with it. He ran only for a few steps, however. An exposed root from one of the big maple trees that lined the sidewalk caught his foot; he tripped, was thrown violently forward, and fell sprawling on his face. He did not relax his hold on the paper, however. It was crumpled, but he held it tightly clenched in his hand.

The fall jarred him considerably. The knee of his trousers was torn and his hand scraped. His hat fell off, and as he slid along the ground on his face, half of his false whiskers were ripped off. He picked himself up as quickly as he could, however, and turned around to see what Lena was doing.

She was nowhere to be seen.

CHAPTER XXIII

UNDER THE LIGHT

Hugh turned quickly and followed the fake detective through the crowd. The man sauntered along as if he was in no hurry whatsoever, so that Hugh too had to walk very slowly. The man stopped and looked in at the windows of many of the stores, and close behind him every time stood Hugh; he was at a loss to account for this behavior on the part of the man he was following, as his dilatory tactics were in sharp contrast to the way in which Lena had hurried.

Every few moments the fake detective took out his watch and looked at the time. Hugh decided he must have an engagement for later on in the evening, and that until then there was nothing for him to do.

As nine o'clock struck on the City Hall clock the man whom Hugh had been following stepped into a drug store. There was a row of telephone booths along one side of the store and the man entered one of these and shut the door. Hugh could see him through the glass, as he took down the receiver and gave the number to central.

Hugh loitered around the store, looking at the various articles offered for sale under the numerous glass

Paul G. Tomlinson

cases, while at the same time he kept a careful watch on the telephone booth. The man talked for what seemed a long time and finally Hugh was afraid to remain in the store any longer lest he should arouse suspicion. He went out and took his stand near the front entrance, in a spot where he could see every one who came in or went out.

There were large posters in the store window urging men to enlist in the army and the navy. Pictures of trim looking soldiers and sailors were on the posters and the cards bore urgent calls for recruits. "Your country needs you *now*," ran the legend and Hugh sighed to think that he was not yet old enough to answer the call. His ancestors had been Americans for many generations, they had fought and bled in every war the country had declared, and Hugh wanted to live up to the traditions they had established. He realized too that his country did need men, perhaps as never before. He knew that in order to defeat Germany every ounce of strength the country possessed would have to be thrown into the struggle. As his father said, "Germany is beaten, but they don't know it yet, and it may take years of stubborn fighting to teach them."

Hugh's thoughts were interrupted presently by the reappearance of the fake detective; he came out of the drug store and turning to the right walked off down the street. He hurried now, so that Hugh had trouble in keeping pace with him. The man walked swiftly as if he had some definite objective in view, and Hugh realized that probably the crisis of the whole affair was not far distant.

Suddenly Hugh spied a rough-looking individual approaching them from the opposite direction; his clothes were dirty and the knee of one of his trousers legs torn. He recognized Bob at once.

The fake detective eyed Bob as he passed, but probably took him for some tramp passing through town; certainly he looked the part. Every one in the crowd edged away from him as he drew near, and Hugh could not help wondering if he looked as tough as his friend.

Bob recognized Hugh as he came along without a word of greeting, turned about and walked along beside him. He had seen the fake detective on ahead and though there was no chance for explanations, he knew that Hugh was still on the trail.

In a few moments they came to the City Hall. The detective looked up at the clock on the tower, compared the time with his watch and then took his stand under one of the electric lights on the street in front.

"He has a date here," whispered Hugh. "We'll have to cross the street."

They crossed over and under the pretense of looking at the billboards in front of the moving picture theater kept watch on their man.

"Where've you been?" demanded Bob.

"Just following that man around," said Hugh. "What happened to you?" and he looked at his friend's torn and dirty clothes.

Bob related the story of his experiences. He had

Paul G. Tomlinson

searched vainly for any trace of Lena and failing to find her had resolved to take one turn along the main street and then go down to the factory. He had met Hugh as has been told.

"But the paper Lena had," exclaimed Hugh. "You got it you say?"

"I certainly did."

"What did it say?"

"Read it," said Bob, handing the crumpled sheet over to his companion.

Hugh started to unfold it, but before he could do so, Bob grasped him by the arm and pointed across the street. "Look," he exclaimed.

A woman had joined the fake detective under the light, and the two were talking together.

"It's Lena!" said Hugh excitedly.

"But where did she come from?"

"I don't know, but there she is all right."

"He's mad about something," said Bob. "Probably because she lost that piece of paper."

"That'll prove to him they're being watched."

"I wonder if they suspect us."

"Let's hope not, yet," said Hugh earnestly. "There they

go," he added a moment later, as Lena and the fake detective started down the street. They still were talking excitedly together and it was hard to tell from their manner whether the man was threatening Lena or pleading with her.

"Another chase, I suppose," sighed Bob. "I'm getting tired."

"Not a chase on foot anyway," said Hugh, for just then the fake detective hailed a passing cab; he and Lena stepped into it and a moment later were being driven rapidly away.

CHAPTER XXIV

AT THE FACTORY

"Well," exclaimed Bob in dismay, "I guess they got rid of us that time."

"Why have they?" demanded Hugh. "Why can't we hire a cab and follow them?"

"Have you got any money?"

"Not a cent."

"Neither have I. I guess we're left."

"Aren't we fools?" cried Hugh angrily. "How could any one be so stupid?"

"There's no use in crying over spilt milk," said Bob. "The thing for us to do is to decide what we ought to do next."

"Let's go down to the factory; I don't see what else we can do."

"All right," said Bob disconsolately. "I do hate to have to go and tell father that we've been tricked and beaten though."

"He can at least get the police to come down and help guard his factory," said Hugh. "Probably no harm will come to it if they do that."

"But how do you know his factory is to be attacked? It may be they are planning other damage to-night. We might have had a chance to stop it if we'd followed those two, and now they've got away from us."

"Your father ought to have reported Lena and Heinrich to the police anyway."

"He said he'd keep watch of Heinie, and no doubt he has. He expected we'd do as well for Lena. We'd better go down and see him about it."

"Let me read this paper first," said Hugh. He once again started to unfold the crumpled sheet that Bob had stolen from Lena.

"You can't read it."

"Why not?"

"Try and see."

Hugh unfolded the paper and gave it one look. "Why it's written in German," he exclaimed in surprise.

"I know it is; that's why I said you couldn't read it."

"We must get it translated."

"Let's take it down to the factory. We can get Karl Hoffmann to tell us what it says."

Without further ado they set out. They walked swiftly and exchanged but few words, for they were both occupied with their own thoughts; a feeling that something was hanging over their heads oppressed the two boys. The country was at war and plotters and spies were abroad in the land. The events of the last two days had convinced them that High Ridge had its share of mischief makers, and they felt sure that that very night a blow would be struck.

A walk of twenty minutes brought them to the factory. The low, brick buildings loomed ghostly in the darkness, with only here and there an electric light burning inside as protection against thieves. The small brick office was situated in front of the other buildings and here a light was shining brightly.

A guard challenged them. Bob recognized the man as one of his father's employees, and soon convinced him that he and Hugh were all right. They passed on and a moment later were in Mr. Cook's office. Mr. Cook was seated at his desk and in a chair opposite him Sergeant Riley was ensconced.

"Well," exclaimed the sergeant as the boys entered, "if ever I saw two hard looking bums you two are it. 'Tis a wonder one of my men didn't run yez in."

"We were sort of afraid of that," laughed Bob. "No one bothered us though."

"Where's Heinrich?" inquired Hugh.

"In the next room," said Mr. Cook. "Where's Lena?"

"We lost her."

"What do you mean?"

Bob told his father what they had done.

"It looks serious," said Mr. Cook thoughtfully. "Sergeant Riley has just come from the hospital and he brought me news of Mr. Wernberg."

"How is he?"

"He's better; he talked a little this evening."

"Did he?" cried Bob eagerly. "What did he say?"

"He didn't talk connectedly," said Mr. Cook. "He was only conscious for a few minutes, and wasn't well enough to hold a real conversation."

"But he must have said something."

"He did. He mumbled about bombs, and plans. He talked a lot about a factory, and kept saying, 'hurry,' over and over again."

"Didn't any one ask him what he meant?"

"I asked him myself," exclaimed Sergeant Riley, "but he was not well enough to answer me or understand what I was saying."

"Do you think he referred to this factory?" inquired Hugh.

"The sergeant thinks so," said Mr. Cook. "There are only two others in High Ridge that they would try to destroy probably, so you see the chance is one in three

Paul G. Tomlinson

that he was speaking of this one."

"I can't imagine a man plotting such things," said Bob bitterly. "He thinks he's helping Germany I suppose."

"Huh," snorted Bob. "A nice kind of man that will earn his living in a country and then try to blow it up. Is he going to get well?"

"The doctors say he has an even chance," said Sergeant Riley.

"Well, all I hope is," said Bob, "that when he does get well they take him and put him in jail for about fifteen years. Have you got plenty of guards, father?"

"I think so," said Mr. Cook. "I've got all I can get anyway."

"Hugh and I are ready to help you know."

"I know it, and I may use you later to-night; we will need them more then probably. In the meantime why don't you go and lie down for a little while?"

"We've got a paper here to be translated first," said Bob.

"Give it to me," exclaimed Mr. Cook. "I'll call Heinrich in."

In response to his summons Heinrich soon appeared from the next room. He looked pale and haggard as though he was tired and worn and worried. He glanced from one to another of the people gathered around the desk, but even his old pals, Bob and Hugh, gave him no more than a fleeting smile.

"We have a letter or something here written in German, Heinrich," said Mr. Cook. "I'd like to have you translate it for us, please."

Heinrich took the paper that was held out to him. Every one watched him narrowly as he looked at it, and were amazed to see him suddenly turn deadly white. His hand shook violently and he had to lean against the desk to keep from falling. He gazed at Mr. Cook pleadingly, a hunted look in his eyes.

"What does it say?" asked his employer.

Heinrich gasped and almost choked once or twice. He swallowed hard and finally found his voice again. "I don't know," he replied.

"You mean you can't read the German?"

That seemed to be as good an excuse as any, so Heinrich seized upon it eagerly. "Yes," he stammered. "That iss it."

"I don't believe you," said Mr. Cook calmly.

"Please, Mr. Cook," begged Heinrich. "Don't ask me to read it."

"But I want to know what it says."

"I can't read it."

"You don't mean that," said Mr. Cook. "You certainly can read it."

"I can't read it," Heinrich repeated. It was plain to be seen that he was suffering great mental agony; he glanced about him fearfully as if he expected to be attacked suddenly. He looked at the paper again and an involuntary groan escaped him. He appealed to Mr. Cook.

"Please let me go home," he pleaded.

"You won't even leave this room until you've read what that says," exclaimed Mr. Cook, becoming angry and irritated at Heinrich's refusal to do as he said. Bob had seen their chauffeur stubborn before, however, and he knew that if he made up his mind to a thing he was as obstinate as only a German can be.

Heinrich merely looked at Mr. Cook sorrowfully.

"I'm a policeman you know," said Sergeant Riley sharply.

Heinrich ignored the implied threat completely.

"Come on, Heinie," urged Bob cajolingly. "Don't be foolish."

"I can't read it," said Heinrich again.

"You know," said Mr. Cook, "we're suspicious of some things you have done already, Heinrich. Don't make it worse if you can help it."

"I can't read it," said Heinrich.

Bob knew the chauffeur well enough to know that there was no use in arguing with him further; it would only be a waste of breath and time.

"I don't want to turn you over to the police, Heinrich," said Mr. Cook. "That is what I shall do, however, unless you do as I ask."

Heinrich turned paler than ever at this, but the words had no other effect on him. "I can't help it," he muttered doggedly. "I can't read it."

"Let me see the paper," said Sergeant Riley. Heinrich handed it over.

"What's the little alligator doing on it?" queried the sergeant curiously.

"Heinrich can tell you," said Mr. Cook. "What does it mean, Heinrich?"

The chauffeur made no reply. He looked at the floor dejectedly but offered no remark. Now and again he glanced about him nervously.

Just at that moment the door of the office was opened and Karl Hoffmann entered. Heinrich looked at the newcomer, and there was hatred in his very glance. His fists were clenched tightly so that his knuckles showed white. He opened his mouth as if about to speak, and apparently with difficulty checked himself.

Karl Hoffmann took in the scene with one glance and was plainly surprised by the gathering. At first he did not recognize Bob and Hugh, who still wore their disguises. Both boys greeted him, however, and laughed at his surprise when he discovered who they were.

Paul G. Tomlinson

Karl himself looked pale as though he was working under a high tension; certainly the times were strenuous. He held something in his hand that apparently he wished to give to Mr. Cook. Before he could speak, however, Mr. Cook anticipated him.

"Here is a paper, Karl," he said. "It has German written on it and I'd like to have you translate it for us if you will."

As Karl took the paper Heinrich started forward as if he would protest. He was pale and his lips were shut tight; his face was the picture of desperation. He looked as if he had reached the limit of his endurance and must speak. For a moment Bob thought he was going to spring at Karl. Heinrich finally got control of himself, however, and relapsed into a sullen calm.

Karl took the paper and looked at it carelessly. Suddenly his jaw dropped and he started back aghast. He turned almost as pale as Heinrich had done.

"Where did you get this?" he demanded.

"Tell us what it says," urged Mr. Cook.

"This is certainly remarkable," said Karl, though by this time he had partly regained control of himself.

"He won't read it, I bet," said Heinrich fiercely.

"Keep quiet, Heinrich!" exclaimed Mr. Cook sharply. "Karl is a good American; of course he'll read. Won't you, Karl?"

"Certainly I will," said Karl easily. He had entirely

recovered his composure now.

He had just opened his mouth to speak when he was interrupted by a volley of shots outside. Instantly everything was in confusion. Every one made a rush for the door and as it was yanked open a piercing shriek rent the air.

CHAPTER XXV

A STRUGGLE IN THE DARK

The woman's scream was so full of terror, so agonized, and so blood-curdling that for a moment the mad rush out of the door was halted. Every one stopped short in horror and amazement.

Sergeant Riley was the first to regain his senses. "Come on!" he shouted and plunged out into the night. Close at his heels followed the others. That is, all except Heinrich; he dashed into the room adjoining the office and remained there unnoticed.

The air was filled with shouts and cries. Men ran hither and thither, black shapes flitting up and down like shadows.

"Spread out!" shouted Sergeant Riley. "Circle the factory and don't let any one escape."

Bob and Hugh unconsciously kept close together in spite of the sergeant's orders. One end of the factory was situated on the shore of the Molton River, and toward the river bank the two boys made their way.

"What a scream that was," shuddered Hugh.

"Awful," cried Bob, and then he tripped over some-thing lying on the ground, and pitched forward headlong on his face. A moment later he had regained his feet.

"What tripped you?" demanded Hugh.

"Look!" said Bob, shivering as he spoke. He pointed to a misshapen heap of something lying on the ground at his feet. "It was soft, like a body."

"The woman who screamed," cried Hugh in terror.

"Strike a match."

"I haven't got one."

"We must pick her up and carry her into the office."

"But she may be dead."

"Suppose she is," exclaimed Bob. "We've got to do it just the same."

"This is terrible," cried Hugh. "Can't we get some one to do it for us?"

"Every one is busy."

"Where's Karl?"

"He's busy, too. Come on, Hugh, we must do it. If she's not dead now she may die while we stand here and talk about it."

Hugh braced himself for the task. They could

Paul G. Tomlinson

distinguish the vague outlines of the woman's form, as Bob stationed himself at her head and Hugh grasped her feet.

"All ready," said Bob. "Lift her up."

"Suppose we are attacked while we're carrying her."

"Lift her up, will you?" demanded Bob angrily. "What's the matter with you, Hugh?"

Bob took hold of her shoulders and Hugh grasped her ankles. She was heavy and absolutely limp so that it was very difficult to lift her from the ground. The two boys exerted all their strength, however, and presently were able to start on their way back to Mr. Cook's office, panting and straining as they went. The distance was not great, fortunately, and soon they opened the door of the office and deposited their burden on the floor.

"Why," gasped Bob, starting back in surprise. "It's Lena."

"What?" demanded Hugh.

"It certainly is. Look at the blood on her shoulder."

"Is she dead?"

"I don't know." He took hold of Lena's wrist and felt for her pulse. "Her heart is still beating," he announced a moment later.

"Hadn't we better get a doctor?"

"I should say so," exclaimed Bob. "Call up Doctor Clarke and tell him to come down here just as fast as he can."

Hugh hastened to obey, while Bob secured a towel soaked in water and began to bathe the wounded woman's face. How had it all happened? Perhaps one of the factory guards had surprised her at some criminal work and had shot her as she fled. Bob did not know enough to understand whether she was badly wounded or not; at any rate she was still bleeding profusely.

Presently Hugh reported that the doctor would be down just as quickly as he could. He had promised to start at once.

"What shall we do?" inquired Hugh.

"Don't you think we ought to stay here with Lena?"

"I don't see that we can do anything for her, and we may be needed outside. Where's Heinie? Why don't we leave her with him?"

"Where *is* Heinie anyway?" exclaimed Bob. He hurried to the door of the adjoining room, but there was no trace of the missing chauffeur.

"He's gone, I guess," said Hugh. "When every one rushed out in the excitement he must have slipped away. We'll never see him again."

"How stupid of us," cried Bob. "Every one clean forgot him, I guess."

"His escape doesn't settle what we have to do," said Hugh.

"Let's go out and leave her here, I say. We don't know anything to do for her. Anyway you told the doctor where to come, didn't you?"

"I did."

"Come on then," and Bob hurried out, with Hugh following close behind.

In front of the office they stopped for a moment, peering intently all about them and straining their ears for every sound. Bob remembered the big hickory stick of his father's and stepped inside again to get it.

"We're taking chances prowling around here unarmed," said Hugh when his friend had joined him once more.

"I know it, but what can we do?"

"Nothing, I guess. Where do you suppose the others are?"

"Let's go find them."

Again they started in the direction of the river, not in a mad rush this time, but slowly and carefully picking their way. They skulked along in the shadow of the factory walls, ready for any emergency that might arise. They kept close together and if the truth were known both boys would have been very glad to have had an armed companion with them.

They had covered perhaps a hundred and fifty feet or

so, and ahead of them could just make out the dark bank of the river. Suddenly they saw a man appear around the corner of the building, running toward them. Bob and Hugh crouched against the brick wall and waited for him to come near. All at once Bob recognized the stranger and started forward.

"Karl," he cried.

The man halted.

"Where are you going?" asked Bob. "Where are father and the others?"

"Down by the river," replied Karl and once more broke into a run. A moment later he was lost to sight in the darkness.

"Seems to me he's in an awful hurry," remarked Hugh.

"Father had probably sent him on an errand," said Bob. "Let's hurry and see if we can't find father and Sergeant Riley."

"Who do you think shot Lena?" asked Hugh.

"I don't know. We'd better not talk here now."

"Do you suppose it could have been the fake detective?" said Hugh regardless of Bob's advice.

"I don't know, but I don't see why he should shoot one of his own gang."

"He blew up Mr. Wernberg though."

"I know it, but I can't understand it, and as I said I don't think we ought to talk here."

They proceeded in silence. Both boys were eager to join the others and they wondered what they could be doing down by the river. Perhaps they had captured the plotter and had dispatched Karl for rope or handcuffs to secure him. At any rate nothing suspicious had happened since the shots had first been heard.

The boys had progressed but a short distance further, when suddenly a great tongue of flame shot heavenward between them and the river. An ear-splitting detonation followed, and the very earth was rocked by an enormous explosion. Both boys were thrown violently to the ground by the force of it, while showers of earth, bricks, and material of all kinds pelted down all about them.

A moment later the boys were on their feet, still partly stunned and undecided as to whether they should run or not.

"There may be another one coming," warned Hugh.

While they hesitated a man suddenly appeared running swiftly away from the direction of the explosion.

"Hey there!" challenged Bob. "Who are you?"

For answer there came the flash of a revolver and a pane of glass in the window close beside the boys' heads was shattered.

"Stop!" shouted Bob at the top of his voice and regardless of danger he started in pursuit of the fleeing man. Hugh was not to be left behind at such a time and together they raced after the fugitive.

Suddenly he stopped, raised his right arm, and hurled his revolver. It struck the ground directly in front of Hugh, spun around a number of times and hit him a sharp blow on his shin bone as it caromed.

"Let it alone," cried Bob.

"It must be empty."

Both boys were fleet of foot, but in the first fifty yards of the race the man gained on them. It was plain to see that unless something happened they would soon be outdistanced. Bob realized that the time had come when chances were to be taken. He raised his father's hickory cane above his head, whirled it around a couple of times, and sent it spinning in the direction of the fleeing figure ahead.

The one chance in a hundred was successful. Bob's aim was true and the heavy stick flew straight to its mark. As the man ran, one end of it protruded itself between his legs; he was tripped up and, losing his balance, fell sprawling to the ground. Almost instantly he was on his feet again, but the delay occasioned by his fall had been almost sufficient to enable the boys to catch up with him. They were barely two steps behind him now.

"Tackle him!" shouted Bob.

Like two ends going down the field to get the quarterback who is receiving the punt Bob and Hugh leaped forward at the same time. They had both had experience in football and it stood them in good stead now. The man went down, both boys literally swarming all over him.

"I've got his legs, Hugh," cried Bob. "Grab his arms."

The man kicked and struggled with all the strength that was in him. Bob hung on for dear life, however. He held one of the man's feet in each hand and threw his body across his legs to hold them down. Hugh scrambled forward and hurled his entire weight across the man's chest. Their prisoner's fists were going like flails, but Hugh persisted. The thought of this German plotting against the United States was more than he could endure and he dealt the man a stunning blow squarely in the face.

A moment later the man's arms and legs were tightly pinned to the ground while the two boys sat astride him, complete masters of the situation.

"I'd like to pound his head off," cried Bob fiercely. "Just look at that fire."

The bomb had done its work, and already the flames were mounting higher and higher over the damaged portion of the factory. The fire whistles were blowing violently; some one had turned in the alarm promptly anyway.

"What shall we do with him?" panted Hugh.

"You didn't knock him out when you hit him, did you?"

"No. He's all right."

"Let's get him on his feet and take him up to the office then."

"Hang on tight."

"Don't worry about that. If he tries to get away we'll choke his head off."

Whether or not the man understood these remarks he offered no comment. Hugh held him by one arm and Bob by the other. They yanked him to his feet and marched him off in the direction of the factory office. Strange to say their prisoner offered but little resistance; he dragged his feet somewhat but followed along sullenly.

Presently there was a clatter and a clang of bells and the fire engine dashed into the yard, shooting sparks in a broad yellow stream from its stack. There was much shouting and giving of orders, and a moment later the hose cart, and the hook and ladder made their appearance.

Whether or not it was the distraction caused by these events, Bob and Hugh never could explain to themselves. At any rate they must have relaxed their caution and paid less attention to their prisoner than they should, for with a sudden violent twist of his body he wrenched himself free and was gone.

Paul G. Tomlinson

CHAPTER XXVI

AN EXPEDITION IS PLANNED

"Catch him! Catch him!" shrieked Bob hysterically.

The man darted away in the direction of the fire engine with the two boys pursuing him at top speed. The fugitive was fleet of foot, however, as had already been proved to Bob and Hugh. He was gaining rapidly on his pursuers, while their shouts and calls were lost in the general hubbub and confusion incident to the fire.

A short distance along the course of the chase two barrels supporting a plank were standing. As the man passed them he hesitated long enough to dislodge the plank and upset the barrels. They rolled directly in the path of the two boys, one of them causing Hugh to trip and fall. Bob kept up the chase, however, but the factory yard was now filled with people attracted by the fire and the man he followed soon eluded him in the crowd.

There was nothing for Bob to do, but give up. He turned back and presently discovered Hugh limping toward him.

"Hurt yourself?" he demanded.

"I skinned my knee. Where's our man?"

"He got away in the crowd."

"We're a couple of fine ones," exclaimed Hugh disgustedly.

"We certainly are," echoed Bob. "I'm getting so I'm ashamed to see father; all I do is report failures to him."

"We'd better go back to the office and see him though."

They returned to the office and at the door met Mr. Cook coming out. He greeted the boys heartily, for he had been worried about them.

"I'm glad to see you two," he exclaimed. "I was afraid something had happened to you."

"Oh, we're all right," said Bob. "Where's Lena?"

"What do you mean?" demanded his father. "I haven't seen her."

"Well, just look at that," said Bob, pointing to a dark stain on the floor. "That's where she was lying; she was the woman who screamed."

"You don't tell me!" exclaimed Mr. Cook. "Was she badly hurt, and who shot her?"

"We can't answer either question. All we know is that we found her outside, unconscious, and brought her in here. She was wounded in the shoulder and bleeding badly. We left her here and went out again."

"Why didn't you telephone for a doctor?"

"We did. We sent for Doctor Clarke."

"And here's a note from him on the table here," exclaimed Hugh. As he spoke he handed the piece of paper to Mr. Cook.

"'Have taken patient to hospital in order to remove bullet,'" Mr. Cook read aloud.

"Golly," exclaimed Hugh. "There's lots going on around here, isn't there?"

"Too much," said Mr. Cook soberly. "I hope that explosion hurt no one."

"How about the fire?" asked Bob.

Sergeant Riley arrived just then and reported that the fire department had the blaze under control and that it was only a question of a short time before it would be entirely out.

"'Tis lucky it is no worse," he said seriously.

"And it's also lucky that my insurance will pay for it all," added Mr. Cook.

"The thing that makes me mad is that the German divils who exploded the bomb all got away," exclaimed the sergeant bitterly.

"Were there more than one of them?" asked Bob.

"We don't know for sure," replied Riley. "One o' the

men told me he saw two of them running away, but he may have been mistaken."

"Well, Hugh and I caught one of them," said Bob.

"You did!" almost shrieked Sergeant Riley, bouncing out of his chair. "Where is he then?"

"We don't know."

"What do yez mean?"

"He got away from us, and we lost him in the crowd."

"Oh, my boy, my boy," wailed Riley, nearly in tears. "Why did yez ever let such a thing happen to you? That was our chance to put a crimp in the whole gang, and now I suppose they'll be after blowing things up worse than ever."

"But we didn't do it on purpose," protested Bob meekly.

"I know yez didn't," said the sergeant. "If I had only been there! I can tell yez that if ever I get my hands on one of them fellers he'll never get away."

"It's too bad," exclaimed Mr. Cook. "Still I don't think the damage they did here will seriously interfere with our work for the Government."

"I hope not," said Sergeant Riley fervently. "I hope yez can make enough ammunition to blow the bloody Germans clean out of France and Belgium and sink every blooming submarine they have on the ocean."

"I hope so, too, Riley," said Mr. Cook. "There's no room in a decent world for people who act as the Germans do."

"First of all though we've got to fix it so they can't interfere with our factories over here," exclaimed the sergeant. "I wish we could catch this gang."

"What happened to Heinrich?" asked Bob. "Did he get away?"

"He did not," said Sergeant Riley. "One of my men escorted him to the police station where he'll be waiting until we want him."

"He didn't say what was on that sheet of paper, did he?"

"Not yet."

"Where's Karl?" asked Bob. "He was going to read it for us."

"I don't know where Karl is," said Mr. Cook. "He hurried off to look after part of the factory just before the explosion occurred. He's a good soul, Karl. I wish all the German-Americans were as loyal as he is."

"Did one of the guards shoot Lena?" Hugh inquired.

"No," replied Mr. Cook. "Karl and I asked them all, and not one of them had even seen her. It's a peculiar thing."

"I wonder if our friend the fake detective could have done it."

"He wasn't the feller you caught, was he?" asked Riley.

"No," said Bob. "Our man had whiskers, didn't he, Hugh?"

"Yes," said Hugh.

"They may have been false," suggested the sergeant. "You've got false ones on."

"And they still itch terribly."

"Why don't you take them off?" inquired Mr. Cook. "I guess you won't need them any more to-night, will you?"

"That depends on what is going to happen," said Bob. "Have you any plans, Sergeant?"

"I wish I had," exclaimed Riley. "What I want to find out is where this gang has its headquarters. When I know that I'll go there and pay a call."

"I know where it is," said Bob.

"You do?" demanded the sergeant in surprise. "What are you two anyway; a couple of young Sherlock Holmes?"

"Not at all," laughed Bob. "We are suspicious of a certain house though, and it might be worth while to go up there and take a look around."

"That's the stuff," exclaimed Riley eagerly. "I'll swear you all in as deputy sheriffs, and we'll get guns for yez and go up just as soon as we can."

"We're only suspicious of this house, you know," said Bob.

"Where is it?"

"Twelve eighty-two Elm Street."

"I heard Heinrich say something about Elm Street," exclaimed Riley. "Your clue may be a good one after all."

"Poor old Heinie," murmured Bob.

"Poor old nothing," cried Riley. "Who feels sorry for a German plotter?"

"But Heinie was stupid and they probably made a fool of him."

"The fact remains, however, Bob," said Mr. Cook, "that Heinrich evidently was in with this gang and therefore he ought to be punished."

"You're dead right, Mr. Cook," exclaimed the sergeant. "No matter whether a man's been made a fool of or not, if he's dangerous he ought to be locked up."

"I suppose so," Bob agreed. "I feel sorry for him though, more sorry than I do for Lena. She has more brains than Heinie and ought to know better."

"Meanwhile we ought to be on our way to Elm Street," exclaimed Sergeant Riley. "Come on, boys, let's get started."

CHAPTER XXVII

A RAID AND A SURPRISE

Mr. Cook's automobile was still standing outside, and a few moments later the little party of four were seated in it and on their way to the police station. Bob was at the wheel.

Upon their arrival it was the work of only a few moments to have Mr. Cook and the two boys sworn in as deputy sheriffs. Bob and Hugh retired to the wash room and after more or less trouble succeeded in removing the false crop of hair from their faces.

Sergeant Riley ordered two policemen in uniform to go with them, and when Mr. Cook, Bob and Hugh had been equipped with pistols and heavy night sticks, the band, now increased to six, were ready to proceed. They used the Cooks' car again and presently were gliding silently along in the direction of Elm Street.

Two blocks distant from number twelve eighty-two Bob stopped the car and every one got out. A short consultation was held and it was decided to separate. Consequently Mr. Cook, Hugh, and one of the policemen went down a side street in order to go around the block and approach the house from the opposite direction. Bob, Sergeant Riley, and the other

Paul G. Tomlinson

policeman were to wait a few moments and then move on up Elm Street. It was thought best to have Bob with one party and Hugh with the other as both boys knew the house and could lead the way with no possibility of mistake.

It was exciting work and Bob and Hugh both felt very important and elated at being allowed to accompany the officers on this raid. Furthermore they were going to see the inside of the mysterious stucco house, and perhaps clear up the whole mystery of the German plot and spy system in High Ridge.

After a few moments' wait Bob, Sergeant Riley, and the policeman started to move slowly up the street. They met no one on the way, for it was now after midnight and people were mostly in bed. Only one house had a light burning as far as they could see; that house was a white stucco one, number twelve eighty-two and the light was on the third floor.

"Here come the others," whispered Bob to Sergeant Riley as they drew near their destination.

Orders had already been given and every one knew what he was to do. One of the policemen went around to the rear of the house and took his position by the back door. Mr. Cook was to guard the front entrance, and both men had instructions to do everything necessary to prevent the escape of any of the inmates of the house.

The remaining four members of the party, led by Sergeant Riley, stole noiselessly up the steps and approached the front door. Riley took a bunch of keys from his pocket, inspected the lock, and then selected one of his keys. At the first trial the lock responded; he grasped the door knob and silently and, with extreme caution, pushed open the door.

The hallway was unlighted. Sergeant Riley took out his flashlight and pressed the button on it for a second as he inspected the hall. He uttered a low grunt of satisfaction as he noted that there was a carpet on the floor, and also on the stairs leading to the second floor. That meant their footsteps would not be heard. He beckoned to the others to follow, and softly stepped inside.

Scarcely daring to breathe, the four raiders advanced. They made no noise on the thick carpet, but a collision with a piece of furniture or a false step might have ruined all their chances for success. Sergeant Riley was in the lead, quick flashes from his pocket torch showing the way.

After what seemed hours they reached the second floor. Thus far nothing had occurred to make them think that they had been discovered, but the hardest part was yet to come. From the third floor came the sound of voices and a shaft of light from an open door pierced the darkness of the hallway. The men above were talking in German.

There was a brief halt and then Sergeant Riley stole forward again. With breath in check and walking on tip-toe his three companions followed. The open door above was about five or six feet distant from the head of the stairs. They started up the last flight; the voices of the men above seemed raised in anger, and though Bob of course could not understand what was said, he thought that the tone of one of them sounded

Paul G. Tomlinson

strangely familiar.

Suddenly the stairs under Sergeant Riley's foot creaked. The little band stopped short, their hearts pounding; every one gripped his revolver a bit tighter and waited for developments. Apparently the noise had not been heard, however, for the voices continued as before.

The advance was resumed and finally Sergeant Riley reached the top of the stairs. He went a little farther and took his stand just beside the opened door and barely out of the light. As the others came up they stationed themselves directly behind the sergeant and close against the wall.

It was a tense moment. Bob and Hugh could feel their hearts hammering so that it seemed to the two boys the noise must be heard. Their faces were pale, and frankly they were frightened. Suppose the men in the room should outnumber them and overpower them? Certainly if they were the spies and plotters they sought, they would be desperate. Then again it was just possible that the men were peaceful citizens, and that the affair would turn out to be a farce; that would be almost too humiliating.

Suddenly Sergeant Riley stepped forward into the open doorway.

"Hands up!" he ordered sharply, covering the inmates of the room with his pistol. His three companions crowded into the doorway alongside him.

There were three men seated about a table in the room, and they were completely taken by surprise. They started to their feet with muttered exclamations of anger and astonishment, staring with wide eyes at the four pistols levelled at them from the doorway.

One man hesitated and made a move as if to reach around towards his hip pocket, but Sergeant Riley was alert.

"None of that," he cried. "Put up your hands."

The man hastened to obey and together the three stood and faced their captors. Sullen and angry they looked, and not one of them spoke.

"Now, Marshal," said Sergeant Riley, speaking to the policeman next to him. "I wish you would be so good as to relieve these gentlemen of any hardware they may have concealed about them."

While Riley and Bob and Hugh covered the three prisoners, the officer went rapidly from one to another and took a revolver from each one of them. He also examined their other pockets, but finding no additional weapons returned to his post by the door.

While this little drama was being enacted Bob had a chance to look about the room. It was scantily furnished, a table, four chairs, and a shelf along the wall constituting its equipment. On the shelf were a dozen or more bottles that looked as if they might contain chemicals; a square black box stood on the table and also a brass spring and what resembled a cord hanging from one side. Bob decided it was a bomb. From a nail in the center of the ceiling a small alligator was suspended by its tail. Bob recognized the missing Percy, and decided that this must be the headquarters of the gang that had used an alligator as its symbol, and traced a picture of it on all the notes and warnings they sent out.

While the furnishings of the room were interesting, the three men captured were far more so, and as Bob saw one of them he experienced a distinct shock. The first was a man with dark hair, weighing perhaps one hundred and fifty pounds, and having a close-cropped mustache; the fake detective beyond a doubt. The second was a thin, wiry individual with a beard, and a swollen, red nose. He was the man who had escaped from his and Hugh's hands at the factory, Bob decided. His nose was swollen where Hugh had hit him. This must be the man who had set off the bomb.

The third prisoner was the one who furnished the surprise to Bob, however. He was a man Bob had known for years, and liked, admired, and trusted as well. He was Karl Hoffmann.

"Well," exclaimed Sergeant Riley, "it looks as if you men was through with your work. Get out your handcuffs, Marshal."

Up till now not one of the prisoners had spoken. When they saw the manacles being brought out, however, they shifted uneasily and Karl spoke.

"Bob," he said. "This is all a mistake."

Bob would have liked to believe him but before he had an opportunity to say anything Sergeant Riley spoke up. "Perhaps it is a mistake," he exclaimed. "We can talk that over down at the police station better than here, however."

There was now little left to do. The handcuffs were quickly attached to the prisoners' wrists and Hugh was sent to the second floor to telephone for the patrol wagon. The prisoners were marched downstairs, and Mr. Cook and the other policeman were summoned. Mr. Cook was as shocked as Bob had been to see Karl Hoffmann among those who had been captured in the raid.

There was nothing for it, however, but to see him loaded into the patrol wagon and driven away to police headquarters.

CHAPTER XXVIII

CONCLUSION

Mr. Cook, with Bob and Hugh, returned home. They had been in the house only a few moments when the telephone rang, and Mr. Cook answered it to find Sergeant Riley on the wire.

"I want to come up and see yez," he said. "I've let one of your friends out of jail and I'll bring him along with me if you don't mind."

He offered no further explanations, and the three friends were at a loss to understand what his visit could mean and who the "friend" might be.

"It must be Karl," said Mr. Cook. "No one can convince me he's disloyal."

"I guess that's who it is all right," agreed Bob.

They discussed their experiences of the past two days, but no one was able to offer any satisfactory explanation for the strange events through which they had passed. There was only one thing of which they were certain and that was that a band of men who were working for Germany had been plotting against the peace and welfare of the United States.

It was not long, however, before Sergeant Riley arrived and every one was greatly astonished to see that his companion was none other than Heinrich.

"Yes," said the sergeant. "Here's your friend Heinrich back again, and I guess he's here to stay this time."

Mr. Cook was a trifle cool in his greeting to the chauffeur. Not that he did not like him, but he had hoped to see Karl with the police sergeant. He had been convinced of Heinrich's guilt, while he had considered Karl to be innocent. Furthermore Karl had been foreman of the factory for a number of years and had proved himself a most intelligent and valuable workman.

"Heinrich has a story to tell you," said Sergeant Riley.

"You confessed, did you, Heinrich?" asked Mr. Cook. He was under the impression that he had confessed in order to save himself, and glad as he was to have the mystery and uncertainty ended he did not like a "tell-tale."

"He had nothing to confess," said Riley. "Tell your story, Heinrich."

"Well," began Heinrich nervously, "in the first place you all suspected me because I worked for Mr. Wernberg. Mr. Wernberg was working all the time for the United States."

"What?" exclaimed Mr. Cook in surprise.

"Yes," said Heinrich, "that iss what he was doing. He knew there was plots on foot and he knew every one in

High Ridge was suspicious of him. He decided to expose those plots and prove that he was a good American. He hired Lena and me mit some others to help him."

"Lena, too, was all right?" demanded Bob.

"Certainly," exclaimed Heinrich. "Of course she iss all right. Mr. Wernberg he knew who these plotters were, but he was not able to prove anything about them. He also knew that they were meeting in that old house out in the woods. The night before last he went out there in a big gray roadster to search the house."

"I didn't know that was his car," said Bob in surprise.

"Yes," said Heinrich, "and I was mit him. You and Hugh followed us and we knew it, so to scare you away I took the automobile and brought it home. You see Mr. Wernberg wanted to do it all himself."

"We couldn't understand it," muttered Hugh. "To think that you were fooling us all the time, Heinie."

"Yes," grinned the chauffeur, "I fool you all right. Well that night we could not find anything so we left and Mr. Wernberg went back the next afternoon to look around. One of the plotter's gang discovered that he was there and tried to blow him up."

"But who locked us in that room?" demanded Bob.

"I did," said Heinrich. "I thought you was part of the German gang."

"Didn't you see us?"

"No, I only hear you talking. Then I fire one shot to give you a scare."

"And you almost blew Bob's head off," added Hugh.

"I tried to shoot high," said Heinrich. "Then I hurry away to tell Mr. Wernberg that I had two of the plotters caught. When I was gone I guess one of the plotters came there and you had a fight with him."

"The fake detective," exclaimed Bob.

"His name iss Kraus," said Heinrich. "He has a little mustache, and in the afternoon he blew up the house, because he knew we were after him and he wished to destroy all evidence."

"That's when Mr. Wernberg got hurt," said Mr. Cook. "What was he doing in the house, Heinrich?" He was amazed at the way the mystery was clearing itself up.

"As I told you," said Heinrich. "He was looking around for evidence against the gang."

"Why didn't he notify the police if he was suspicious?"

"As I told you," repeated Heinrich patiently, "he wished to do all himself and when he turned those men over to the police no one could say he was forced to do it. They sent him lots of warning notes because they knew he was after them."

"What did the alligator mean?"

"It iss the sign of a secret society; all Germans in High Ridge know that. It was that snake Hoffmann who stole poor Percy to kill him and hang him up in the room where they had their office."

"How long has Karl been a member of the gang?" asked Mr. Cook.

"Ever since Germany went to war with England," said Heinrich. "Nearly three years."

"But he never talked as though he sided with Germany."

"The ones who mean trouble never do," said Heinrich. "Karl knew enough to keep his mouth shut. You see you never suspected him."

"Tell me about Lena," exclaimed Mr. Cook. "Why was she meeting that man Kraus down town tonight and going around with him if she was not working with the gang?"

"She pretended to Karl Hoffmann that she was working mit them. All the time she was acting as a spy for Mr. Wernberg. Because Karl Hoffmann was in love with her he told her lots of things, and it was in that way we got most of our information."

"Pretty clever, eh?" exclaimed Sergeant Riley, approvingly.

"There's another thing, Heinrich," said Mr. Cook. "Why wouldn't you read what was written on that paper tonight?"

Heinrich looked sheepish. "I could not," he said. "Kraus had become suspicious of Lena; he feared she was going to betray them and the note was a warning to her. It said that if they were caught they would see to it that she went to jail mit them. At that time you were all suspecting poor Lena, and I was afraid you would send her to jail before she had a chance to prove to you that she was loyal."

"You're in love with Lena, aren't you?" asked Mr. Cook.

"We are to be married," said Heinrich, proudly, his eyes shining.

"Did Karl suspect that Lena was treacherous?"

"I think not until he saw that note."

"He was going to read it to us though."

"He would not have read it," cried Heinrich hotly. "He would have made up something, not what it said at all."

"Who shot Lena?"

"Kraus shot her. She was going to your office to warn you that your factory was going to be blown up, and he shot her to prevent that."

"Who was the man with the whiskers?" asked Bob.

"His name iss Mueller. He iss the one who set off the bomb tonight."

"That's what we thought," exclaimed Bob. "Well, Hugh, you hit him one good one anyway, didn't you?"

Paul G. Tomlinson

"I hope so," said Hugh.

"There was four of them altogether," said Heinrich. "Kraus, Mueller, Hoffmann, and a man named Schaefer who went to blow up the railroad bridge Friday night and has not been heard of since."

"We know where he is, don't we, Hugh?" laughed Bob.

"Where iss he?" demanded Heinrich.

"In jail, I guess," said Bob. "We caught him on the bridge with a bomb."

"Good boys," said Heinrich warmly.

"Why were you so angry when you had to go with father tonight?" asked Bob. "Where was your engagement?"

"I was going with Lena to twelve eighty-two Elm Street, where Schaefer lived. You see Lena was already a member of the gang, so they thought, and I was to join too, so we both could watch them better."

"Somebody telephoned Lena about meeting them there this evening."

"Yes, it was Mueller. He thought he had a recruit in me."

"Well, Heinrich," said Mr. Cook, "I guess that explains pretty nearly everything, and I'm sorry I ever suspected you." He shook hands warmly.

"Oh, that's all right," smiled Heinrich. "I had to get

suspected with the job I had. That was part of the game."

At that moment the door bell rang and Dr. Clarke was ushered in. "I thought you might be interested in the hospital patients," he said. "Mr. Wernberg will recover all right, and Lena is not badly hurt. She keeps calling all the time for somebody named Heinrich. Do you know him?"

"Will you excuse me, Mr. Cook?" exclaimed Heinrich, and, without waiting for a reply, he dashed out of the room, nearly falling over two chairs in his haste to get away to the hospital.

"He seems to be in a hurry, doesn't he?" laughed the doctor.

"I must be going, too," said Sergeant Riley. "I have some boarders down at my hotel who may need attention."

"Well, good-night, Sergeant," exclaimed Mr. Cook, shaking hands with the doughty officer. "I'm sorry Hoffmann was mixed up in this business, but I'm glad it's all cleared up. I hope we'll have no more trouble."

"Ye won't, as long as yez have two young fellers like Bob and Hugh working for yez," exclaimed Riley. "The United States needs boys like that; this war is going to be a long and hard one in my opinion."

"I'm afraid so," Mr. Cook agreed. "I guess we'll come out all right if we all work hard and stick together though."

"That's it," exclaimed Riley. "We must all work together. Our personal feelings don't count. It's what our country needs."

He said good night all around and went out.

* * * * *

The next morning Bob was out in the yard inspecting a plot of ground where he was going to have a garden. He could not enlist, but he was going to "do his bit" by raising a few vegetables, and thus help to supply the country with its necessary food. He heard a step behind him and turned to see Frank Wernberg.

Frank held out his hand. "Shake hands with me, Bob," he exclaimed. "I want to tell you that I was wrong about that the other day, and you were right."

Bob responded heartily. "Yes," said Frank.

"I was dead wrong. I had thought from the way father talked that he was pro-German, but I found out that he wasn't at all. When it came to a question of deciding between his country and Germany there was never any doubt about where he stood."

"I know that, Frank," said Bob. "I wish every one of German birth or descent over here felt the same way."

"I think most of them do," said Frank.

"I guess that's right," Bob agreed. "Look at Lena and Heinrich."

"Well, all I wish now," exclaimed Frank, "is that we

could enlist."

"So do I," cried Bob enthusiastically. "Wouldn't it be wonderful if you and Hugh and I could enlist and go together?"

The new adventures are recorded in the story entitled,

BOB COOK AND THE GERMAN AIR FLEET.

Choose from Thousands of 1stWorldLibrary Classics By

Adolphus WilliamWard
Aesop
Agatha Christie
Alexander Aaronsohn
Alexander Kielland
Alexandre Dumas
Alfred Gatty
Alfred Ollivant
Alice Duer Miller
Alice Turner Curtis
Alice Dunbar
Ambrose Bierce
Amelia E. Barr
Andrew Lang
Andrew McFarland Davis
Anna Sewell
Annie Besant
Annie Hamilton Donnell
Annie Payson Call
Anton Chekhov
Arnold Bennett
Arthur Conan Doyle
Arthur Ransome
Atticus
B. M. Bower
Basil King
Bayard Taylor
Ben Macomber
Booth Tarkington
Bram Stoker
C. Collodi
C. E. Orr
C. M. Ingleby
Carolyn Wells
Catherine Parr Traill
Charles A. Eastman
Charles Dickens
Charles Dudley Warner
Charles Farrar Browne
Charles Ives
Charles Kingsley
Charles Lathrop Pack
Charles Whibley
Charles Willing Beale
Charlotte M. Braeme
Charlotte M.Yonge
Clair W. Hayes
Clarence Day Jr.
Clarence E. Mulford

Clemence Housman
Confucius
Cornelis DeWitt Wilcox
Cyril Burleigh
D. H. Lawrence
Daniel Defoe
David Garnett
Don Carlos Janes
Donald Keyhole
Dorothy Kilner
Dougan Clark
E. Nesbit
E.P.Roe
E. Phillips Oppenheim
Edgar Allan Poe
Edgar Rice Burroughs
Edith Wharton
Edward J. O'Biren
John Cournos
Edwin L. Arnold
Eleanor Atkins
Elizabeth Cleghorn
Gaskell
Elizabeth Von Arnim
Ellem Key
Emily Dickinson
Erasmus W. Jones
Ernie Howard Pie
Ethel Turner
Ethel Watts Mumford
Eugenie Foa
Eugene Wood
Evelyn Everett-Green
Everard Cotes
F. J. Cross
Federick Austin Ogg
Ferdinand Ossendowski
Francis Bacon
Francis Darwin
Frances Hodgson Burnett
Frank Gee Patchin
Frank Harris
Frank Jewett Mather
Frank L. Packard
Frederick Trevor Hill
Frederick Winslow Taylor
Friedrich Kerst
Friedrich Nietzsche
Fyodor Dostoyevsky

Gabrielle E. Jackson
Garrett P. Serviss
Gaston Leroux
George Ade
Geroge Bernard Shaw
George Ebers
George Eliot
George MacDonald
George Orwell
George Tucker
George W. Cable
George Wharton James
Gertrude Atherton
Grace E. King
Grant Allen
Guillermo A. Sherwell
Gulielma Zollinger
Gustav Flaubert
H. A. Cody
H. B. Irving
H. G. Wells
H. H. Munro
H. Irving Hancock
H. Rider Haggard
H. W. C. Davis
Hamilton Wright Mabie
Hans Christian Andersen
Harold Avery
Harold McGrath
Harriet Beecher Stowe
Harry Houidini
Helent Hunt Jackson
Helen Nicolay
Hendy David Thoreau
Henrik Ibsen
Henry Adams
Henry Ford
Henry Frost
Henry James
Henry Jones Ford
Henry Seton Merriman
Henry Wadsworth
Longfellow
Henry W Longfellow
Herbert A. Giles
Herbert N. Casson
Herman Hesse
Homer
Honore De Balzac

Horace Walpole
Horatio Alger, Jr.
Howard Pyle
Howard R. Garis
Hugh Lofting
Hugh Walpole
Humphry Ward
Ian Maclaren
Israel Abrahams
J.G.Austin
J. Henri Fabre
J. M. Barrie
J. Macdonald Oxley
J. S. Knowles
J. Storer Clouston
Jack London
Jacob Abbott
James Allen
James Lane Allen
James Andrews
James Baldwin
James DeMille
James Joyce
James Oliver Curwood
James Oppenheim
James Otis
Jane Austen
Jens Peter Jacobsen
Jerome K. Jerome
John Burroughs
John F. Kennedy
John Gay
John Glasworthy
John Habberton
John Joy Bell
John Milton
John Philip Sousa
Jonathan Swift
Joseph Carey
Joseph Conrad
Joseph Jacobs
Julian Hawthrone
Julies Vernes
Justin Huntly McCarthy
Kakuzo Okakura
Kenneth Grahame
Kate Langley Bosher
L. A. Abbot
L. T. Meade
L. Frank Baum
Laura Lee Hope

Laurence Housman
Leo Tolstoy
Leonid Andreyev
Lewis Carroll
Lilian Bell
Lloyd Osbourne
Louis Tracy
Louisa May Alcott
Lucy Fitch Perkins
Lucy Maud Montgomery
Lydia Miller Middleton
Lyndon Orr
M. H. Adams
Margaret E. Sangster
Margaret Vandercook
Maria Edgeworth
Maria Thompson Daviess
Mariano Azuela
Marion Polk Angellotti
Mark Overton
Mark Twain
Mary Austin
Mary Cole
Mary Rowlandson
Mary Wollstonecraft
Shelley
Max Beerbohm
Myra Kelly
Nathaniel Hawthrone
O. F. Walton
Oscar Wilde
Owen Johnson
P.G.Wodehouse
Paul and Mable Thorn
Paul G. Tomlinson
Paul Severing
Peter B. Kyne
Plato
R. Derby Holmes
R. L. Stevenson
Rabindranath Tagore
Rahul Alvares
Ralph Waldo Emmerson
Rene Descartes
Rex E. Beach
Richard Harding Davis
Richard Jefferies
Robert Barr
Robert Frost
Robert Gordon Anderson
Robert L. Drake

Robert Lansing
Robert Michael Ballantyne
Robert W. Chambers
Rosa Nouchette Carey
Ross Kay
Rudyard Kipling
Samuel B. Allison
Samuel Hopkins Adams
Sarah Bernhardt
Selma Lagerlof
Sherwood Anderson
Sigmund Freud
Standish O'Grady
Stanley Weyman
Stella Benson
Stephen Crane
Stewart Edward White
Stijn Streuvels
Swami Abhedananda
Swami Parmananda
T. S. Ackland
The Princess Der Ling
Thomas A. Janvier
Thomas A Kempis
Thomas Anderton
Thomas Bailey Aldrich
Thomas Bulfinch
Thomas De Quincey
Thomas H. Huxley
Thomas Hardy
Thomas More
Thornton W. Burgess
U. S. Grant
Valentine Williams
Victor Appleton
Virginia Woolf
Walter Scott
Washington Irving
Wilbur Lawton
Wilkie Collins
Willa Cather
Willard F. Baker
William Makepeace
Thackeray
William W. Walter
Winston Churchill
Yei Theodora Ozaki
Young E. Allison
Zane Grey